THE LAST STAND OF FATHER FELIX

Also by Leonard Wibberley

Mrs. Searwood's Secret Weapon
Stranger at Killnock
The Quest of Excalibur
Take Me to Your President
McGillicuddy McGotham
Beware of the Mouse
The Mouse That Roared
The Mouse on the Moon
The Mouse on Wall Street
A Feast of Freedom
The Island of the Angels
The Hands of Cormac Joyce
The Road from Toomi
Adventures of an Elephant Boy
The Centurion
Meeting with a Great Beast
The Testament of Theophilus

NONFICTION

The Shannon Sailors
Voyage by Bus
Ah Julian!
Yesterday's Land
Towards a Distant Land
No Garlic in the Soup
The Land That Isn't There

JUVENILES (FICTION)

Deadmen's Cave
Kevin O'Connor and the Light Brigade
The Wound of Peter Wayne
John Treegate's Musket
Peter Treegate's War
Sea Captain from Salem
Treegate's Raiders
Leopard's Prey
Flint's Island
The Red Pawns

JUVENILES (NONFICTION)

Wes Powell—Conqueror of the Colorado
The Life of Winston Churchill
John Barry—Father of the Navy
The Epics of Everest
Man of Liberty—the Life of Thomas Jefferson
Young Man from the Piedmont
A Dawn in the Trees
The Gales of Spring
Time of the Harvest

LEONARD WIBBERLEY

THE LAST STAND OF FATHER FELIX

WILLIAM MORROW & COMPANY, INC.
NEW YORK 1974

Printed in the United States of America.

1 2 3 4 5 78 77 76 75 74

Library of Congress Cataloging in Publication Data

Wibberley, Leonard Patrick O'Connor (date)
  The last stand of Father Felix.

  I. Title.
PZ4.W632Las [PS3573.I2] 813'.5'4 74-3441
ISBN 0-688-00285-4

Chapter
One

THERE are so many stories circulated about him these days
that it is time to set the record straight insofar as I can.
The stories range from impossible reports that he was
raised from the dead to equally impossible reports that he
deserted the priesthood to save his life and is still alive
in a remote part of what was formerly a Portuguese colony
in East Africa. I frankly confess, to start with, that there
are men in Africa and elsewhere who knew him far better
than I, who, a newcomer, knew him only in his old age.
But I was with him in the last days when the mystery
surrounding him began. I can testify to those days and
when I have given you the whole story perhaps you can
make up your mind concerning what happened to him.
Everybody in Mombasa fifteen years or so ago knew

Father Felix. Mombasa is a funnel through which all the exports of Kenya, Tanganyika, the old Belgian Congo and Uganda flow. With them flows all the news from these parts, for the vast area comprised by the term "East Africa" is, even these days, despite all its new states with new names, really a huge village. It has its village personalities, some quite unknown to the outside world and not necessarily people of political or economic importance.

Skinner, for instance, with his scrawny figure, the right shoulder always thrown a little forward, his pathetically big hands and his shocking red hair. Skinner was known all through East Africa and sure of a meal, a drink and a bed wherever he went, though nobody could say what he did for a living.

He told me once that he was an agent ashore for Arab dhows, and certainly he spoke more Arabic dialects than many Arabs. But what he meant by "agent" he wouldn't define, and, the mores of that vast village of East Africa forbidding direct questioning, I never found out.

Then Grossheimer, my fellow American, with his thin legs and his vast belly and shoulders. His business was quite open. He was in the lumbering business, cutting what was left (quite a bit actually) of mahogany, camphor and sandalwood, in areas where he could obtain permission to cut and where he could put in a road to bring the timber out. Grossheimer was a wealthy man and a figure of economic importance. But what he was known for was his beetle collection. Yes, he had the most astonishing collection of beetles ever brought together—drawer after drawer of them—beetles with claws on them like lobsters; beetles so tiny that they were visible only under a magnifying glass when they glowed in myriads of colors like a good opal.

Grossheimer became interested in beetles, when he first arrived in Mombasa, as a result of the war which we Americans have waged for so long against insects. Other peoples of the world, by and large, have learned to live with insects; but Americans have not. And Grossheimer, meeting the Mombasa cockroach for the first time, attacked it with New World fury and finally came to admire its ability to survive gasoline, arsenic, naphtha, DDT and starvation. He began to regard cockroaches, and by extension all beetles, as the equal of humanity, and finally to hold them superior.

His beetle collection was not only fascinating but it was also frightening. There are far, far more of them than there are of us. They are far more varied and much, much tougher, and appear to be increasing both in number and variety. The conclusion is inevitable that if beetles ever learn to think, we are finished. (Grossheimer held that they are already beginning to think in a terrifying fashion of their own.)

Father Felix was a different kind of village character, more solid, more permanent, more patriarchal. Everybody knew, for instance, that Grossheimer must one day explode with apoplexy, briefly mourned by the silent, tender, young girls who flitted about his house overlooking the bay. Everybody knew that Skinner would one day be buried at the expense of the British community in the European cemetery at Mombasa. But nobody ever thought of an end for Father Felix, directing the tiny Mission of the Sacred Heart in the remotest part of Blemi, itself, even in Africa, a remote part.

The mission lay on a fringe of heavy forest on the east bank of the Blemi river. Between the mission and the coast lay vast thickets of those thorns called "wait a bit," and beyond, extending for mile on mile along the coast, were even worse thickets of gray-green and stinking mangroves, from which the Arabs, in season, cut staves to load in their dhows and carry to the markets of the Persian Gulf.

Father Felix was then cut off by thorns, by forest and by mangrove from the rest of the vast village of East Africa. He was for over fifty years the voice crying in the African wilderness in that mission which he had built himself in that remote part for the precise reason that it was remote and therefore in greatest need of a mission. And because of his remoteness and his heroic devotion to his work, Father Felix came to represent in Mombasa, in Zanzibar and in vast areas of Kenya and Uganda and Tanganyika (I use the old names, you see) the missionary presence of the One Holy Catholic and Apostolic Church. When you thought of Catholicism you didn't somehow think of the Bishop of Nairobi, for instance. You thought of Father Felix, stuck out there between the thorns and the forest teaching generations of little black children about the Holy Ghost, Michael the Archangel, Mary the Virgin Mother, plenary indulgences, saints' days, holy water, processions, prayers for the conversion of Russia and so on. All that huge accretion of two thousand years of Catholicism was not embodied in the Bishop of Nairobi playing golf or the Bishop of Nairobi confirming scores of neatly clad black children. It was embodied in the tall figure of Father Felix, who spoke Blemi and Watta, Swahili and Arabic, but continued to say his daily Mass in Latin despite the directives of ecumenical councils, the chidings of bishops and the exasperation of his immediate superior, Canon Kronk.

Father Felix was a figure in East Africa, and his conservatism gained him great popularity, at least among the whites, who in that part of the world admire conservatism. He had some surprising allies and supporters, many of them of no particular religion at all. Among the more surprising of these was Robinson, the Glasgow Scot, who had a huge collection of pointless but quite irreverent jokes about priests and nuns. "Father Felix is an ignorant, stubborn, guid mon," he said to me once and immediately asked, "Did ye hear the one aboot the skinny nun and the bishop's son?" Stories of this sort were the cross that Robinson had to carry, but the trouble was that those in his company had to carry it too. Robinson was, however, an excellent surgeon, though the way he spoke of the human body would make you doubtful of letting him slaughter a pig.

I met Father Felix for the first time in the billiard room of the Shamrock Club in Mombasa. At the time he would have been in his late seventies. The Shamrock Club is a seedy sort of place, its membership largely consisting of ex-civil servants, most of them British. Many of these had retired in East Africa, and those who didn't like the isolation of the hinterland and couldn't afford Nairobi or Zanzibar migrated to Mombasa. There, unless they had lavish means, they all joined the Shamrock Club, which was housed on the third floor of a hotel overlooking the harbor. It had a reading room, a billiard room, a library, a bar and a verandah. In the library you could find fairly recent copies of the *Illustrated London News*. In the bar you could get a glass of India Pale Ale instead of having to drink bottled Simba beer, which isn't English.

I had just finished a game of billiards when Father Felix came in; tall, commanding and dressed in the white robe of the Dominicans, which didn't quite hide the pair of khaki slacks below or do much to cover a pair of thick boots, suitable for duck-hunting in Canada. He had, of all things, a white solar topee in his hand and a monstrous Gladstone bag in the other. His whole appearance was so incongruous that I thought one of the members was putting on an act. I had had one pony of whisky too many and I went up to him and said, "Dr. Livingstone, I presume?"

"Livingstone?" he said quite seriously. "No. Father Felix. Of the Sacred Heart Mission," as if the Sacred Heart Mission was as well known as St. Peter's in Rome.

Having made such a gaffe, I apologized, introduced myself and asked him if he would join me for a drink. He nodded and seemed a trifle bewildered, like a man uncertain of his surroundings and not at all sure of how he came to be in them. I steered him to one of the basketwork chairs on the verandah, where above the scent of dried salt cod, which is Portugal's gift to the whole tropical world, the tenuous sea breeze brought an occasional whiff of lime blossoms, sweet and cleansing. He ordered a Simba—"The beer of lions"—and, fumbling with his hand, produced from somewhere beneath his white robe a small black coin purse out of which he fished, with thick fingers, a British half crown.

"It's on me," I said. But he put the half crown on the top of the table between us, keeping a finger on it until the boy came with the drinks. Then he lifted it up, between finger and thumb, and handed it to the boy, as if he were offering Communion.

"The gentleman is paying, Father," said the boy reverently and even affectionately.

"Thank you," said the priest to me. "But I only want one and I had saved this out for that purpose."

So I said, "Thank you, Father," and let him pay. He seemed pleased. It's hard, I suppose, to be the constant object of charity and courtesy—never to be allowed to pay for yourself, or take a buffet or two.

"Cheers," I said, raising the lime crush I had ordered to do battle with the whisky, but he ignored the toast and took quite a copious drink of his beer, refilling the glass from the bottle which had been placed on the table top.

"Livingstone," he said, harking back to my gaffe. "He died a little while before I was born. But I knew some of the boys who were with him on the banks of the Lulimala where he died. That was in old Chitambo's village. The day before he died, he was so weak he could hardly wind his watch. He did that every morning, you know. They found him dead, kneeling at the foot of his bed, and put the body out in the open to sun-dry and preserve it. It was in May. The dry season."

He told the story with such detail, such intimate knowledge, that he gave the impression that he had been present. He knew the names of the blacks who had laid out the body and the porters who had carried it, sun-dried and wrapped in cloths, across Africa to Zanzibar. He described the procession of tattered blacks coming out of the interior with the mummy of the "Great Master" carried on their shoulders on poles. "Even the Arabs followed the procession," he said. "Even the Arabs. He was buried a year later in Westminster," he added with regret. Plainly when it came to his own burial, he wanted no grave in a dusty cathedral, but interment in the great edifice of Africa.

Father Felix had come to Mombasa on this occasion to hunt up some supplies for the mission which had been lost somewhere in the Customs warehouse. He warmed up to the subject of these supplies. "Six new banners," he said. "From Italy. In silk. The Sacred Heart on a white background and the Immaculate Conception. I found them in the Customs shed. I have them with me. Would you like to see them?"

He dug into that impossible Gladstone bag, brought them out and held them up for my admiration. The one of the Sacred Heart showed a huge red heart, big enough for an elephant, which had been converted into a kind of vase from which there proliferated, not flowers, but flames. The massive red heart with a huge wound in it from which monstrous drops of blood fell down the white of the banner was so grotesque as to be almost laughable. The other banners were less spectacular; representations of the Virgin Mary holding the infant Jesus in her arms with a circle of stars around her.

I was embarrassed and didn't know what to say. The banners irritated me—more than that, they angered me. Ten generations of Protestant ancestry rose in my gorge to protest against the outrageous Catholic display. But the tall old priest was utterly unaware of this reaction and I was saved by the club servants, who came over to murmur their approval and delight, including Selim Abdul, who was in charge of the Billiard Room and whom I knew to be a Moslem and therefore an enemy of all images. So, taught good manners by a Moslem, I said that I thought the banners were striking and he folded them up carefully and put them away in his Gladstone bag.

He was greatly relieved to have found the banners and thought them well worth the prolonged journey from Blemi, part of it by dugout indifferently propelled by a tiny Seagull outboard and a few paddlers, part by pony and the rest by road on a native bus stuffed with blacks and Indians, surrounded by crates of chickens and baskets of cassava and yams and sweet potatoes and stems of bananas and plantains. He was the only European aboard.

"They have to keep urinating," he said. "Yaws." That little detail illuminated the whole journey for me: the heat, the flies, the squalling children, the screeching hens and the frequent stops while one or another of the passengers of the jolting, rocking bus got off to squat by the roadside.

I questioned him about life in Blemi for, after all, I am a journalist and he was a source of vast knowledge about a remote part of a Portuguese colony, itself remote.

There was progress, he said. Definite progress. The number of baptisms was up and there were more children attending the mission school. I inquired about sleeping sickness, yaws and beriberi. His face took on a tired look but he assured me that there was progress. Large areas were quite clear of tsetse. Mortality among infants was much lower now, only about ten percent, according to the later figures. "Less than New York," he said. "Much less than New York."

"But, Father," I protested, "I am sure the New York figures on infant mortality are much below ten percent."

"You're forgetting abortions," he said. "You can't ignore abortions." I thought this view outrageous and sputtered some kind of protest. He didn't listen to me but busied himself refolding his banners.

He went off then, extending to me first an old worn hand whose loosely joined bones moved under my handshake. He picked up his solar topee and his broken-down Gladstone bag containing the banners of the Sacred Heart and the Immaculate Conception triumphantly rescued from the Customs warehouse and strode across the room

[17]

and out the door. As he went I thought of the old hymn
we used to sing so proudly in the days of my youth—

> Onward, Christian soldiers,
> Marching as to war,
> With the Cross of Jesus
> Going on before. . . .

Chapter Two

I was in Mombasa to collect material for a series of articles on smuggling; all kinds of smuggling—ivory, heroin, guns, hashish, pearls. Ease of communication has produced a vast increase in smuggling these days, enlarging at one and the same time the market and the means of access to it. The jetliner works with the ancient seagoing dhow in promoting the smuggler's business, and the gentlemen in the four-hundred-dollar Italian silk suits who have never seen an opium poppy are partners of the ragged Turk, Iranian or Indian peasant collecting the sticky juice in the hope of a few piastres or rupees.

I don't want to libel Mombasa by pretending that it is a hotbed of smuggling. There is far more smuggling, I am sure, in New York or San Francisco, to pick two names at random. But Mombasa is a glamorous place and Pittsburgh, for instance, isn't. And one of the principles of journalism is that it is better to have an exciting setting for your story. A man would have to be dull indeed not to be able to get a highly salable series of articles out of Mombasa.

I liked Mombasa. I liked the Jesus fort, standing on the grassy mound overlooking the harbor, with the initials "I.H.S." carved in the walls by the Portuguese who built it four centuries ago. I liked the Arab harbor where the last of the world's working sail gathers—the big baggalas or seagoing dhows with their high sterns carved in the manner of long-gone Portuguese caravels (it was the Portuguese who taught the Arabs this art). Then the graceful sambuks and the India kotias, and so on. They crowd into their own part of the harbor—ships from India and Persia (I hate the name Iran) and the Arabian principalities, clustered together in the gin-clear water, floating on their own reflections and manned by Moslems who at the appointed hours stop all they are doing to say their prayers.

Lord, the grace, the presence, the aliveness of that scene! And what an exultation when a deepwater boom comes sweeping in from a long voyage, leaning under her vast lateen sail, with everybody aboard banging drums and gongs and chanting, and leaving to Allah, who has presided over the whole voyage, that last perilous mile full tilt into the heart of the anchorage.

I spent a lot of time in the dhow anchorage, and got to know a number of the quartermasters and pilots on the various vessels, as well as the agents ashore and the Customs people and the immigration people. But though everybody assured me that there was smuggling, nobody could or would give me any details. So I settled down in

Mombasa to wait, for it is an axiom of journalism that the story which you cannot track down will often come to you if you will be still, watch and listen.

I rented a bungalow in the English quarter, close to the ocean, and got the right number of servants and joined the right clubs and drank the right drinks and so on. I joined the Shamrock Club, where I met Father Felix. But I also joined the Lusitania Club (more exclusive) and it was there that I met Grossheimer with his beetles, and there at the bar that I one day found, to my great surprise, Skinner, his huge red hand encircling a vast planter's punch, his right shoulder thrust forward, and examining on the bar top a few drops of water which had dripped off the iced glass he was holding.

Skinner was the last person one expected to see at the the bar of the Lusitania Club. He wasn't a member. He couldn't afford the fees, to start with, and he just wasn't the type who would be admitted to membership. I assumed that he was a guest of one of the members, who had taken him in charge for the while and been indiscreet enough to bring him into the club—a new member, then. I was surprised when Major Anano, the British Political Officer, joined him, took a glance at the still-unfinished planter's punch and discreetly ordered one drink for himself. He caught sight of me and frowned. Political officers do not like journalists, but the frown was immediately replaced by a little smile about as warm as winter sunshine and he beckoned me over.

"You know Skinner, don't you?" he said. "Just back from the bush with all kinds of interesting stories, aren't you, Skinner?"

Skinner emerged from the drops of water on the bar and said, "Found out anything about heroin?"

[21]

"Nothing," I said. "But I'm not choosy. Ivory will do. Or guns."

At the word *guns* Anano sniffed his whisky glass tentatively and took a cautious drink. "There's guns all over the bush," he said. "Not just what survives from the Mau Mau. We've got most of them. These are new. Czech and Russian mostly, but some Austrian. And lots of ammo. We've known it for a long time. What we didn't know was where they came from and how they got there."

"And you know that now?"

Anano shook his head. His head always reminded me of a huge cube of lard with a black mark which was his moustache in the center. "Officially no," he said. "As a matter of fact, officially I suppose we never will know. There are many, many things that you never know officially." He glanced at the clock over the bar and said, "Well, I must be off," and, picking up the little riding crop which he always carried, he touched it to his forehead and was gone. It was (besides his little waxed moustache) his only vanity. Anano, a Syrian by race, though British-born, had for a short time been in the Household Cavalry. That was the apex of his career. I heard that he had only been a trooper, but the fact that he had been in the Household Cavalry at all provided him with the status needed to overcome his Syrian birth in the British caste system.

"Bye," he said and was gone, leaving me with Skinner. The barman, a Parsee, glanced at us with an air of superiority and disapproval. He could not himself ask Skinner to leave the bar now that his host had gone. It would be unheard of for an Indian to tell a European to get out. But he could and would send a message to the club secretary, a peevish little Lancashire man who sported a Winchester tie, and he would ask Skinner to leave.

So, to solve the problem, I suggested to Skinner that we drink up and go and have a meal at my bungalow, where I would be delighted if he would spend the night in return for telling me more about guns and the bush and anything else that came into his head. On the way to my bungalow I reflected that it had been very bad manners on the part of Anano to leave his guest with me, and then decided that, for political reasons of his own, he wanted me to pump Skinner about guns and their source.

We had curried lobster, cold beer and Arabian coffee spiced with ginger for lunch (excellent for the digestion) and Skinner told me about the guns. They were, he said, "everywhere." It turned out that by everywhere he meant mostly in Blemi and the country to the south. They were modern, some of them those high-velocity machine pistols which fire a .22 slug with such speed that it instantly disintegrates when it hits a twig or even a leaf. You can imagine what happens when it hits something more solid like a man.

"Or an elephant," said Skinner. "Makes a hole you could put your head in."

"Surely that isn't the object?" I asked. "Guns for hunters? Meat and ivory?" The question wasn't as foolish as it sounds. The big need of the African is protein. He just can't get enough meat. Anthropologists say that is the reason some of them were cannibals and I believe the anthropologists are right. An elephant is a lot of meat, and when you've been eating mealies and cassava and yams and a few river fish that taste like mud for months and a herd of elephants goes by, it's almost impossible to resist those mountains of steak. Even the blood tastes good.

Skinner considered my question carefully and, dipping his finger into his glass, made a little pool of water on the table before him. He was fascinated by little pools of water.

"They use them for cutting down trees too," he said slyly. "The headman calls everybody and then he lets off magazine after magazine, watching the splinters fly, and at last the tree shivers and sort of glides to the ground, picking up speed and moaning."

"Moaning?" I said.

"The wind in the branches when it falls," he said. "Then everybody gets the hell out of there because there's usually half a dozen snakes, mad as hornets, not to mention centipedes and flocks of tarantulas—the gingery ones that look like hairy crabs."

"Elephants and trees," I said. "Stop stalling. What else?"

Skinner gave me a grin. "Target gets bigger all the time, don't it," he replied. "Like to guess?"

"The white man?" I asked.

"Bigger, I said," said Skinner. "You're getting smaller."

"I didn't think you were a cynic," I countered.

"I'm not," said Skinner. "But when you look at the white man around here in Mombasa or anywhere else you find him in any numbers, he's no size at all. He's kind of like ants. Just numbers and business. No. The bigger target is—well, it's hard to say. It's all this," and he waved his hand about my bungalow and indeed embraced the city around and the harbor below.

"The twentieth century," he said. "That's it. The twentieth century and the nineteenth and the eighteenth.

Africa for the Africans. That's the ticket. Africa for the Africans and the hell with Livingstone."

It was so odd that he had said "Livingstone" that for a while I just stared at him in silence.

Chapter
Three

IT TOOK me three days to get all that he knew about gun-running into Blemi out of Skinner. He wasn't unreluctant to tell me, but he had a completely disorganized mind. One of his failings was that he assumed that I was acquainted in detail with the geography of Blemi and he would refer to places like Draki's Village or Thompson's Crossing or the Ugala Swamp as if they were as familiar to me, by name at least, as Columbus Circle or the Golden Gate Bridge or Piccadilly Circus.

Again, he assumed that I knew the people in these places and would talk about Ramashwar and Hedeker and Prescott as if they had been my neighbors all my life. So I had to keep stopping him and asking him who was Ramashwar, and where was Thompson's Crossing and so on. He would explain impatiently and then plunge on because all these people and places were so real to him that he just could not understand why they were not real to me. Skinner had about a dozen books in him that would make the best of Rider Haggard read like children's nursery tales. The trouble was that he couldn't organize his material, or even link it together with any coherence, and he could hardly tell it. I struggled with him for three days and out of it all I got was the following mishmash.

The guns were coming from Russia. My heart sank when Skinner insisted on this, because, like you, I have long ago given up any belief I had in the Communist Menace. Oh, it's real enough, I suppose, as is, from the Communist point of view, the Capitalist Menace. But it has been so overplayed that anytime anybody blames anything on "the Russians" or "the Communists" I automatically just don't believe it. And I didn't believe it when Skinner said that the guns were coming from Russia. I said, "Malarky." And then I added, "And I suppose that all through the bush are Communist agents readily recognizable by the fact that they speak with a thick accent and wear round fur hats."

"Round fur hats?" said Skinner. "What for? In that heat?"

"Maybe they've got snow on their boots," I countered.

Skinner shook his head and said sulkily, "If you don't want to believe me, it's a waste of time my saying anything, isn't it?"

"I've just had it on that Communist stuff," I said. "Did Anano put you up to this? How do you know the guns come from Russia?"

"You going to write all this up?" said Skinner, ignoring the questions. "If so, leave my name out of it."

"You automatically become a 'reliable source,'" I replied. "But I repeat—how do you know the guns come from Russia?"

"Well, they're Russian make," said Skinner. "Or Czech, which is the same thing." It isn't but I let that go. "And then there's the way they are brought into the country."

"And how are they brought into the country?"

"Some from the Congo. Some by dhow."

That stopped me. I thought of a deepwater dhow calling in at Archangel up in the Arctic Circle or maybe at one of the Black Sea ports and loading up with cases of guns and ammunition, and all but decided that Skinner had been too long in the bush this time, had seen one or two automatic rifles in the hands of headmen and turned the whole thing into a Communist plot to seize Blemi, the one part of Africa that nobody has ever wanted because of the flies, and turn it into a Red Satellite. Believe me, even the Belgians, who at one time snapped up everything they could find in Africa (with the British, Germans and French), had turned down Blemi, and though the place was officially a Portuguese possession, that represented only a color on a map.

"It's the Israel-Arab business, you see," said Skinner seriously. "Up the Kwale River as far as the crossing and then across the Cabo strip. . . ."

"'What the hell has the Israel-Arab business got to do with it?" I demanded.

"Christ," said Skinner. "And you a magazine writer! You Yanks have thrown in your hand with the Israelis and that leaves the Arabs to the Russkies. Prescott's been hanging around. . . . I had a beer with him in Maikap."

I stopped him and beat out of his amorphous mind the following. There was, he admitted, no actual Communist plot to take over any portion of Africa or any of the

African republics emerged or emerging since the end of the Second World War and turn them into Russian satellites. The Russians had decided, however, to counterbalance the growing strength of Israel, backed by the United States, by supporting the Arab states and supplying them with arms of all kinds.

But they did not want an Arab war with Israel because they were afraid it would get out of hand and involve the whole East and maybe the whole world.

This I thought ridiculous and said so, for I couldn't see the whole East, or any substantial part of it, going to war because of a dispute between Israel and the states of the Arab Union.

"You don't understand what an Arab is," said Skinner earnestly. "You think an Arab is something like an Englishman or an American. He's not. When you think of Arab think of Moslem and then you can think of North Africa, East Africa, Egypt, the Sudan, Iran, Turkey, Pakistan. That's what I mean about getting out of hand."

The plan was to keep up pressure short of war in Israel and start trouble elsewhere to distract the attention of Israel's allies, especially the United States. So the big dhows were bringing Russian guns down from the Red Sea ports and dropping them off here and there along the East African coast, but principally in Blemi, where control was lax or lacking and where the dhows went anyway, to flounder up the Blemi river into the mangrove and fill their holds with poles to be sold in the Arabian market, where lumber of any kind is utterly non-existent.

I didn't believe a word of this rigmarole. Oh, I believe that maybe a case or two of guns had been run into the back country by the Arabs, or had drifted down from the Congo, but I didn't swallow what it seemed to me on reflection was Major Anano's Great Russian Plot to Spread Rebellion in East Africa, and I was amused (and irritated) that he should have thought he could dupe me with Skinner's rambling tale.

I met Anano later that week on the third hole of the golf course, where you drive off across the wind, which is always fluky, with a large water hazard slightly to leeward. My drive was good. A little upwind of the fairway, with just a short iron to the green, and Anano said, "Nice. American clubs, I suppose."

"No," I replied. "Made in Moscow and smuggled in by Arab dhow."

He gave me his winter-sunshine smile and wandered off in the direction of the clubhouse. I think he blushed. But at least he understood what I thought of Skinner's carefully planted tale of Russian guns all over the African bush.

I was playing with Grossheimer that day and he invited me up to dinner, which meant that in return for looking at case after case of his beetles, I would get an excellent meal and the only cup of genuine American coffee to be found east of Ambrose Light. I accepted the invitation to get away from Skinner, who was still staying at my bungalow and getting on my nerves with his disconnected mind. We had Jerusalem artichokes, smoked salmon and fresh, crisp salad, and the beetles didn't bother me so much. In fact I became mildly interested in them, though Grossheimer's emphasis on their being the largest single order in the animal kingdom, with 250,000 known species identified by 1945 (he'd identified three new species himself), left me bored for I had heard it so often. Still, he had a huge new beetle to show me—*Dynastes hercules* (I wrote the name down) a little over six inches long—and

[*31*]

another whose camouflaged back looked like dead moss and its antennae like dried-up vine tendrils.

"Cunning," he said. "Terrifyingly cunning. The beetles run things much better than we do. They have no morals, which is one reason. They can dive, swim, fly, jump, send messages by voice or by flashing lights, store food, camouflage themselves, make drug addicts of bees and ants so as to steal their food and young, and survive on nothing—absolutely nothing." He produced a piece of glass tubing sealed at both ends with something inside.

"Beetles," he said. "I sealed them in there nine months ago with some dried coffee beans. Still alive. See for yourself." They were still alive.

"That one," he said, "is carnivorous. It's a diver. It catches fish and it has hollow tubes in its jaws through which it sucks the body fluids—like a vampire."

Seeing ahead of me two solid hours of beetles I became almost panicky after a while and said, right out of the blue, "Have you heard of Anano's Great Russian Plot to Seize Blemi?"

"No," he said. "I haven't."

So while he opened up case after case of beetles, and interrupted me by producing specimens—one, for instance, from Borneo that is used in both embroidery and jewelry-making—I told him the story, all very badly jumbled up, I'm afraid. When I had finished, his mind was still on his wretched beetles and I said I had to leave because Skinner was alone at the bungalow.

He offered to drive me home, but I said I'd sooner walk. He did see me to the end of his garden, heavy with the scent of wild ginger, and as we parted he said, "All around us. Millions of them. Tunneling, chewing, biting, digging, eating, killing, building, signaling. And whenever

[32]

we see one, we just step on it. Just *think* of that—we automatically step on it. As if it were some kind of a race instinct."

I walked slowly home through the warm, moist night, with the scent of jasmine, citrus, salt fish, cloves and an occasional whiff of sour coconut oil from the harbor about me. It occurred to me that everybody in the world probably has his own particular touch of lunacy. It is this touch of lunacy that keeps us all sane, for pure, unadulterated, machinelike sanity would drive us mad—is, in fact, madness. The thing, of course, is to keep all in balance and not let our little eccentricity go too far. Grossheimer was teetering on the edge.

Amused with the thought, I looked about for further examples. My own little abnormality consisted, I decided, in a habit of talking aloud to myself when alone. It relieves my feelings, particularly if these are concerned with embarrassment or shame. Sometimes, remembering some clumsy or cruel thing I said or did years ago, I will cry aloud, "Oh, what am I to do?" And anyone who heard me would think I was mad. Like Grossheimer, I have to watch it. Anano preserved his sanity by playing the part of an officer of the Household Cavalry, and poor old Skinner, always hinting at some dramatic and mysterious development in the bush, loved little pools on table tops and peered into them like a fortune-teller with a crystal ball. Skinner's little play pools, I thought and laughed aloud.

When I got home, Mrs. Blair, my housekeeper, told me that Skinner had left, which was really a relief. She was a widow in her fifties, her gray hair caught in a bun at the back, and the muscles of her face sagging. Her husband, who had been a marine engineer down at the. harbor, had died of drink and general rot years before and was buried in the European cemetery. They were from Glasgow—Greenock, actually. She spoke about Glasgow as if it were the center of the world for kindness, good sense, proper administration, honesty, decent bread and everything else desirable in mankind. She couldn't go back to Glasgow, however. She stayed in Mombasa to tend her husband's grave. That was her particular form of madness.

Chapter
Four

WELL, I was utterly and completely and entirely wrong
about the Great Russian Plot to Spread Rebellion in East
Africa, though I don't think it was Russian. Because two
months later Blemi erupted in rebellion and the whole
vast village of East Africa, from the lakes to the Indian
Ocean and from Somaliland to Southern Mozambique,
buzzed like an overturned beehive. Everybody remembered the Mau Mau revolt in Kenya and everybody saw
immediate and terrifying parallels. Everybody said they
had expected something of the sort all the time and the
damned Portuguese, with their ill-treatment of the na-
tives, were to blame, though that didn't explain the Mau
Mau eruption in Kenya.

The first reports told of bungalows set afire and crops
destroyed. The Gary family—father, mother and two

young children—had been killed, though they offered no resistance to the attackers. They just came out of their bungalow as ordered, frightened and anxious, Mrs. Gary carrying a tablecloth she had been embroidering, and they were cut down with burst after burst of automatic rifles, such an unnecessary outpouring of fire that the body of one of the children was completely cut in two. The heads were then placed on stakes, so the story went, reminding me of the appalling climax in Conrad's *Heart of Darkness*.

The news flew about the country by telegraph and by radio, and among the blacks in the bush by drums. All over the bush the drums started talking and they were the more menacing for isolated families of Europeans because they could not understand what was being said. Then some of the names that Skinner had tossed out at me, as if I and everyone else in the world knew who they were, began to become familiar.

Prescott was one of them. It evolved that Prescott was an Englishman who had been a prominent soldier of fortune in Morocco and Kenya and the Congo—a mercenary, in short—one of the breed who sprang into being at the end of the Second World War. He was now reported as a leader of a Republican Blacks Army in southern and western Blemi.

Then Draki. Skinner had referred to Draki's Village in some connection which I had forgotten. Well, it seemed that Draki was the headman of a village on the Tanganyika border where the old Bantu stock still prevailed. He was the Keeper of the Drum—that is, the sacred drum of the Bantu people, which had been given them by the spirits of their ancestors at the time of the first Hamitic invasion. Don't ask me when that was. Nobody knows because in much of Africa there is no measurement of time in years but only by generations, as was once the case among the Jews.

Whether this drum actually existed could not be known for sure because it was sacred and not to be seen by white men.

At the Lusitania Club there was an old gentleman, Turpington, who sat most of the day on the verandah in a basketwork chair, looking as if he were carved out of old ivory, and who was said to have seen the drum. I never got up enough nerve to ask him whether this was so. You can't just walk up to a graven image, invade its particular level of existence (which may indeed be beyond your reach) and ask it a question which is prompted only by idle curiosity.

Whenever I passed Old Turpington out on the verandah, I had the feeling that I ought to make some kind of gesture of reverence because I had the impression that he was something more than a human being. I don't know how old he was. People guessed at ninety but I thought that ridiculously short of the mark myself.

Anyway, Draki was now emerging as the ethnic leader of his people, the Messiah of the Bantu, who would reestablish their racial supremacy in Blemi and Tanganyika. Since he was a chief, his supporters came to be known as Royalists, opposed, of course, to the Republican blacks.

In any other part of the world it would be ridiculous to suppose that a people so suppressed, so lowly, so lost as the Bantu should aspire to reconquer their old territory. But in Africa the past is far more important than the present. There had once been a race of fighting Bantus who had come up from the south, sweeping aside every opposition. The sacred drum promised the return of that

[37]

race, and the bush boys, whom you could see shuffling around in their khaki shorts on great bare feet, doing all the longshore jobs in Mombasa and Zanzibar, grinned to each other as they humped the huge sacks of cloves and copra about the docks, and knew far more about the drum and Draki than Anano and his whole network of informers and agents.

There were about half a dozen episodes in which bungalows were set afire, plantations burned and the owners slaughtered, on the Blemi-Tanganyika border in Draki's territory. The British authorities sent troops to the border and helped those refugees who escaped what was obviously a race war, with some nasty atrocity stories attached to it. The world loves primitive people now. It is a sentimental fashion and that fashion ignores the fact that primitive man, whether Ancient Briton, Indian or African, gets a great deal of satisfaction out of torture.

The British could not, of course, send troops over the border to put down the revolt. That would have been to invade Portuguese territory. One British column was reported to have crossed over and penetrated to the outskirts of the village of Hako five miles inside the Blemi border. Then the lieutenant in charge prudently withdrew and afterward explained that he had become lost—not so silly an explanation since at that point the border is unmarked and the country round about in the dry season is a wasteland of thorn bushes, rough grass and miserable red dust.

The revolt was a Portuguese affair—as the Portuguese chargé d'affaires in Mombasa pointed out. It had not been unexpected, he said (the work of Communists, of course), and Lisbon was already taking the measures needed to cope with it. But the measures needed to cope with it were somewhat slow in getting underway and the next we knew was that the Portuguese governor and his staff turned up in Zanzibar, having deserted Maikap, the capital of Blemi, which was seized by the "Republicans," and the Republic of Blemi was proclaimed with one Utori as its President.

Utori. All right. It was another of Skinner's names. I would like to make the point that it is curious how, when a revolution takes place, names previously unknown suddenly become familiar to the world, and one finds it a little hard to think back to the time when they were unheard of. Then, of course, especially in the case of Africa, they are in a little while utterly forgotten. Test this on yourself. Who was Tshombe? Is he alive or dead? Who was Lumumba, and Munongo, and Muke, and even Kenyatta, the Aristotle of—was it Kenya?

My point is that these names spring upon the world and everybody becomes familiar with them and then all but a few wither away. Out of Blemi there now came a list of such names—Draki with his Sacred Drum, and Bantu supremacy holding sway in the northeastern region where the mountains rise and the tropical forests are replaced by glades of tree ferns and impossible shrubs twenty and more feet high and related to the daisy family; Utori in the south and west, who had been several times to Lisbon (he was educated at a select private school in Coimbra) and had been assistant to the Secretary of the Governor in the old Portuguese administration; then Colonel Santos, who finally made himself head of the royalist mercenaries by the simple process of insuring that they all got paid; and Schwartz and Prescott and the Arab Mahoud Ibrahim and on and on. I can only think of such people as mushroom spores, waiting for a particular dew to fall so that they can overnight spring into being. The dew in their case was, of course, blood.

[39]

In any case, six weeks after the first report of the outbreak the Republic of Blemi was proclaimed, and a little later Major Anano one evening dropped by at my bungalow and, after accepting a drink and tapping a cigarette to his satisfaction on the silver case he carried in the breast pocket of his semimilitary shirt, asked me whether I would like to meet Utori.

"My dear Major," I said, "not even a commission from *Time-Life,* accompanied by a large check, would ever persuade me to go to Blemi. I have inherited a small family burial plot in Hartford, Connecticut, and I intend to be buried there."

"Utori is here in Mombasa," said Anano smoothly. "Unofficially, of course. I thought that since you rather messed up the story of the golf clubs from Moscow"—he was not without a sense of humor—"you might recoup a little ground by interviewing Utori."

This stopped me, but with Anano it was always advisable to proceed cautiously. His motives were strictly political, never altruistic. "The golf clubs aside, what's the angle?" I asked.

"Nothing at all, old chap," said Anano. "Just a friendly gesture. Person to person. You've been here rather a long time without much to write about, I'd say. Thought it might be helpful."

"Would you say, unofficially, of course, that the British government was rather more interested in the establishment of Utori's Republic than in Portugal regaining control of Blemi?" I asked.

"I would say, unofficially, of course," said Anano through a wreath of cigarette smoke, "that the British government is interested as a matter of general policy in promoting the legitimate aspirations of peoples everywhere to self-government. Of course," he added, "Portugal is our oldest ally but, like ourselves, no longer able to support her many commitments abroad. And a Bantu rising . . ." He didn't finish the sentence.

"What's wrong with a Bantu rising as opposed to any other kind of rising?" I asked.

Anano shook his big block of lard of a head. "You Americans," he said with sorrow. "You blunder so badly everywhere. It's because you're detribalized, and so you cannot think in tribal terms. But just think of tribes for a moment. Africa is not a nation—it's only 'African' in the cities, and there it's European. Out in the bush it's a network of tribes with white overlords. Now if once one of those tribes, thrusting off the white overlords, of course, succeeds in any kind of self-government effort, all the rest of them will start stirring. Think of the effect. The Masai, the Zulu, the Hamites—I'm talking of big ethnic groups, not the interrelated groups like the Nyamwezi and the Wangoi and the Ama-Zulu—think of them all deciding to reassert themselves, to reclaim their territory and reestablish their customs in a war of murder, as in Kenya. To put down that kind of thing (and it would have to be put down) you'd have to wipe out whole populations and leave the corpses stinking in the sun. Far better, far more humane, far more efficient, a reasonable, untribal Republic—if there has to be a revolt at all."

I wasn't impressed and said so. I said the British had a thing about tribes—a hangover from their massacre of the Scottish and Irish clans in the seventeenth century.

"My dear boy," he said. "Tribal wars are horrifying. I am not just thinking of the status in Africa of Europeans. We're outsiders. Also, we are no more friendly to one tribe than the other. But if the Bantu, under Draki with his Sacred Drum, were to succeed in Blemi, his government, to justify itself, would have to make slaves of, or kill off, the Waturi and the Sambara and even the Blemi. And we just can't have that, can we?"

But an education in the radical-liberal atmosphere of Princeton and Columbia is not to be fooled by such thinly disguised Limey imperialism. "I suppose," I said sarcastically, "that before the white man came to Africa, the whole continent just seethed with tribal warfare, with prisoners captured and enslaved, and perhaps eaten by the hundred thousand?"

"Good God," he said, "how else do you suppose Hawkins and the rest of them got all the blacks to send to your country as slaves?"

I must admit that, for the moment, he had me there.

Chapter
Five

UTORI received me with every evidence of pleasure and a confidence in my influence in the United States as a journalist which was flattering but also, alas, naive. There are only two or three magazines which have any real impact on the American conscience, whose articles create any lasting impression on their readership. One is the *Reader's Digest* and another is the *National Geographic.* I had never written for either of them.

Utori from the start, however, was anxious to get an article in *National Geographic,* which would be a sort of exploration of Blemi, its geography and peoples on the one hand and, on the other, a lasting plug from a highly respected magazine for his new Republic. He thought all I had to do was submit to a guided tour through the country and take thousands of color pictures of smiling people, clean villages, pretty girls and children behind golden mounds of King oranges, mangoes or flowers, get it into the *National Geographic* and he would have the sympathy and support of the solid part of the American public. I told Utori that it was highly unlikely that the *Geographic* would accept a piece from me on Blemi.

"How about a bribe?" said Utori. "Supposing I offered them a nice sum of money?" He was wonderfully frank, and I liked him immensely for it.

"Listen," I said, "you can't expect to succeed offering a bribe to a newspaper, a magazine, or even a journalist. Not because they are necessarily so honest, but because the reputation they have for integrity is worth far more than any bribe you could come up with."

"A pity," said Utori, "for I was about to offer you a bribe and also the post of my personal press secretary, with a salary of five thousand dollars a month. Payable into a Swiss bank of your choice, in advance. You wouldn't even have to pay income tax on it."

Really he was a very engaging fellow. He was one of the very few blacks who had not only absorbed some Western culture but also some Western humor and sophistication. He wasn't a big man, but small and dapper, his woolly hair touched here and there with white, giving him a lot of dignity. His face was small and shiny, his nose being the only arresting feature, for it was one of the flattest I've ever seen, tending to confirm rumors I heard later that Utori was from the Congo and a member of one of the small, high-bush tribes.

We got along famously. He had the one characteristic which I think is common to all great men: the ability to be candid. He said the policy of the Republic, under his presidency, would be to follow the Western lead and modernize the whole country. He had no patience with people who talked about preserving the culture of the tribes, the ancient ways, the pastoral life, the loyalty to chiefs and fetishes and phases of the moon and so forth.

"Those who talk like that are deliberately planning the continuing enslavement of the African peoples while pretending to wish to preserve them," he said. "Would the English and the French and the Germans like to be still living in mud huts, taking perilous journeys in boats of animal skins, enduring summer flies and winter rains all for the sake of being true to their culture and picturesque? Of course they wouldn't. The people who talk so sentimentally about these things live in lovely houses, work in air-conditioned offices, have schools, hospitals, roads, beaches, parks, post offices, telephones and every other convenience readily available to them. When all these things are as readily available in Blemi, I will tolerate nostalgic talk about the good old days of the thatched hut and the simple village life."

"There is such a thing as urbanization and overcrowding," I said. "If you were to even smell the IRT subway in New York at rush hour you'd know what I mean."

He grinned. "I've smelled it," he said. "Wonderful. A very small price to pay. Have you noticed how very, very few of those pushed, jostled, deafened and faceless New Yorkers ever move to Wyoming when they retire—or even go there for a holiday? No, my dear sir. All this talk about the pastoral life, closeness to Nature and so on, is a luxury of a completely modern urban civilization. In the case of Africa, and Blemi in particular, it serves only to keep us in the Stone Age, while you, talking nostalgically of primitive simplicity, start to explore the planets.

"When I was a young man, I adored colonialism and I

[45]

loved Portugal. I thought that Portugal would rescue us from the Stone Age at last, turn us into Homo sapiens instead of leaving us Cro-Magnons. I went to Portuguese schools. I studied hard. I entered the government service and obtained a position of eminence. And gradually, indeed against my will, I came to see that the whole colonial policy was designed not to advance us but to use us to the fullest extent, while never allowing us to get into the twentieth century.

"The best we could hope for would be to be incomplete Portuguese. Or to put it another and better way, incomplete human beings. Hominoids, doing the work but never fully sharing the benefits—the real rewards. So, reluctantly, I have had to throw out the Portuguese. They are not only no more use to us, they are a hindrance to further progress."

"Well," I said, "I never heard that Blemi was a shining example of beneficial colonialism. But I know that there were some excellent schools of every grade maintained by the Portuguese even in Blemi to educate the blacks—give them the highest possible European education if that is what they were looking for. You yourself benefited from those schools."

"So sad that those schools should have all failed," said Utori.

"You think they failed?" I asked.

"Yes, indeed. Just think. Out of those schools there came not one single black capable of running a mine or a railroad or an accounting office or a government department. Not one. Like me, the very best of them wound up in third-grade posts, carrying out policies decided from above by nonblacks—filling out forms, adding up figures, filing pieces of paper. Now, for such a failure in education there can be only one of two explanations. Either the schools were no good, and that cannot be admitted, for they were excellent and staffed entirely by fully qualified teachers, I assure you of that. Or the pupils were stupid. And after all, as they say so often, how can you take a Stone Age mind, my good sir, and with just one generation of teaching turn it into the mind of a modern executive? Think of all that accretion of superstition; all the hundreds of thousands of years of abysmal, animallike ignorance. How are a few years of school going to overcome that?" He laughed, quite genuinely, without any bitterness whatever.

"Really, that argument which I have heard so frequently is almost convincing," he said. "Except that it is scientifically absurd, for the human mind is the human mind, and its thought patterns are not hereditary and so formed at birth, but are learned from experience. It is true," he added, "that a white man's brain on the average weighs a few grams more than a black man's brain. But that is a mere matter of quantity, and when you are my size, you soon learn to ignore quantity and concentrate on quality."

Yes. He had a good sense of humor and I liked him. He said he probably wouldn't have launched his revolution at the time he did if it hadn't been for Draki.

"He forced my hand," he said. "Because Draki and his Sacred Drum and his Bantu Nationalism are at war with the twentieth century. He is trying to push us right back to where we were when the Portuguese took over and brought us the little way they have."

"Why, then, didn't you leave the Portuguese to put down the Draki revolt?" I asked. "If you yourself weren't ready."

"It would have meant allowing them to bring so many

[47]

troops into the country that my own plans for revolution could not have succeeded," he said. "And then there was the happy chance of Tupper's convoy."

"That's one story I haven't heard," I said.

"I'm telling it for the first time. You can tell it to the world. You see the advantages of working with me—an endless supply of exclusive revelations?" He smiled and went on. "Tupper's is a monthly convoy coming out of the Congo at Albertville and then down the lake to Lipili—well, never mind the route. It's well known. The trucks carry mixed cargoes—salt, skins, palm oil, guano, indigo, ground nuts, ivory . . ."

"Ivory?" I queried.

"Twenty thousand elephants a year," said Utori. "They raise hell with crops, you know. It's deplorable but it isn't so deplorable if a herd of them has just destroyed five hundred acres of your standing crops. Like your American buffalo, symbol of the freedom of the Great Plains, et cetera. So sad that they are now no more. But can you imagine free-roving herds of buffalo flowing across the cornfields of Kansas and trampling everything flat? Out of the question. Everybody agrees. So why is everybody suddenly defending the elephants? When there are as few elephants left in Africa as there are buffalo in America, we too, I assure you, will deplore the slaughter of the herds and preserve the survivors. By then, like you, we will be in a position to do so. We will have millions of acres of corn and cotton and sugar cane. We will have arterial roads and cities and miles and miles of railroad track and airports. We will be well clothed, well housed, well schooled and well fed, and then we can say, with misty eyes, once there were great herds of elephants—such a pity—" He broke off smiling.

"Look," I said. "I'm of the opinion that somewhere

[48]

along the way we, whom you want to copy, were wrong. That we put physical convenience before less tangible but equally important values. For that reason our civilization, which you so admire, is full of psychiatrists, cocktail guzzlers, glue sniffers, pot smokers, astrologists, all trying to stop the pain. But the pain doesn't stop. Somewhere, my friend, we made a mistake."

"What a lovely mistake," said Utori. "You mustn't be selfish, you know. We have a right to make it too."

To return to Tupper's convoy, it appears that when it finally got among the perilous mountain roads into Blemi, it was stopped and found to contain cases of automatic rifles, hand grenades, plastiques and even (ridiculously) one hundred bayonets.

"For ceremonial purposes, I suppose," said Utori. "They were bound for Draki's Village. They were seized and diverted to Maikap under the guard of a Portuguese sergeant and half a dozen soldiers. Black. It was all kept secret. I knew of it and it wasn't very hard to arrange to blow up a bridge and capture the convoy once it was out of Draki's territory. Once that was done, there was no road back. We had crossed the Rubicon (actually it was the Simili), and the revolt was launched."

"And just who is behind you?" I asked.

"Everybody in Blemi who is second class," said Utori smoothly. "All the second-class clerks, assistant overseers, secretaries to the assistants to bureaus, the overtaxed headmen, the underpaid mine workers and lumbermen. Everybody who is black and who isn't a Bantu."

"That last sounds a little tribal, which I thought was something you opposed," I said.

Utori frowned. "Draki has forced tribalism on me," he said. "Draki has forced me to use the tribal weapon. He has united the Bantu and I have to unite all the non-

Bantu tribes. Otherwise I'd be ignoring, for a principle, a supply of fighting men I just can't afford to be without. But the Republic *is* national, not tribal. Members of any tribe, irrespective, will and do now hold office. The Bantu will be welcome once their revolt is over and Draki has been deported. He won't be killed or imprisoned. He'll just be pronounced insane and sent to India or someplace. He can't be allowed to become a hero."

He rubbed his flat, puttylike nose about his face with a fist—a gesture which indicated he had just thought of a joke. "Even the white tribes will be welcomed in the Republic," he said. "Provided they will forget their tribal affiliations."

"There is a difference between a tribe and a nation," I said.

He was serious immediately. "Yes, there is," he agreed. "A tribe is much, much stronger. Do you know why? It's their myths. Yes. Their myths. The Sacred Drum of the Bantu. And the Golden Stool of the Ashanti. And if you want to take it a tiny bit further there is the sacred rock of the Arabs at Mecca, and the sacred manger of the Christians in Bethlehem."

"Well," I said, "all you have to do in your case is get the Bantu Sacred Drum and demonstrate that it's just an ordinary drum and there's nothing sacred about it."

"Wouldn't work," said Utori. "I'm surprised at you. No. I have to educate them. Myths are things you have to educate people out of—not deprive them of. I have to overcome them physically and then I have to reshape their minds. A very hard job indeed. But it can be done. Education can overcome anything—don't you agree?"

"Everything but humanity," I said. "And they're working on that."

Chapter
Six

THE Utori interview I sent to *The New York Times Magazine* and it was reprinted in the London *Observer* and *Figaro* and in newspapers all over South America and even in the Johannesburg *Drum*. They all carried my by-line and very soon I was, ridiculously, an expert on Blemi and was getting inquiries from Reuters and from Associated Press and from *Time-Life* and heaven knows what for stories, articles, fill-ins, backgrounders and the rest on every aspect of the Blemi revolt. Could I get a similar interview with Draki—this from *The New York Times*. Could I cable two thousand words on arms smuggling—this from the *National Observer*. Could I send three thousand words and pictures on slave running? (King Features.) I was only saved from this deluge of inquiries by the arrival of several special correspondents in Mombasa who soon found that Zanzibar, with its more extensive night life, was a much better place from which to cover the story and took themselves off there, to become, each in his own way, an expert on Blemi.

Utori was very pleased with this result. He had come to Mombasa to get all the financial, economic and political support he could for his Republic. He had avoided Zanzibar because rumor of his mission had preceded him (I learned later) and everybody was looking for him there—particularly the Portuguese. He went back by dhow, which was the way he had come, landing at the little port of el Khalil and turning up triumphantly in Maikap very pleased with himself.

Anano told me that. You've got to hand it to the British. At first you despise them, but after a while you have to admire them. I had taken Anano, on first acquaintance, for a stuffy fool, with a heavy mixture of snobbery. But after a time I began to suspect that that was all a disguise—the riding crop and the Household Cavalry stuff, I mean—and that inside that lardlike head there was a brain, subtle enough to have thrived in the courts of the Borgias.

I hadn't gone for the Great Russian Plot story with the interior of Blemi bristling with guns brought in by Arab dhows. On reflection I decided that Anano had intended that I shouldn't go for it and had laid it on thick and used Skinner's simple mind as his instrument. Then, when Blemi blew up, which it did, I was more ready to accept his offerings, of which the first was Utori. It wasn't comfortable to realize that I was becoming, without my agreement or even my knowledge, a tool of Anano and the British Foreign Office. Yet I had to admire the way he managed it. To salve my pride I let him know that I knew I was being used. He listened to me carefully and patiently and said, "What you ought to do, old chap, is get an interview with Draki. Sort of balance the thing up and establish your neutrality as it were."

"Is Her Majesty's government about to change sides?" I asked.

"We haven't any sides, old boy," he said calmly. "We're through with that sort of thing. But, after all, one does need a rounded picture. So much of public opinion is based on a one-sided view these days, you know. Actually Draki is not a bad sort."

"You know him?" I asked, surprised.

"Yes. We had him in jail for three years. That was in Kenya."

"What for—subversion?"

"No. Eating a three-year-old child. To restore his vitality. He's getting on, you know."

"Three years for cannibalism?" I exclaimed.

"Ah well, if it were *you*, of course, you'd have been hung. But you have to take the background into account. You see, what is cannibalism for us was just medicine for him. The funny thing was that when we let him out, he *did* look younger. Something to do with enzymes or other queer little creatures, I think."

I thought he was pulling my leg, as the British say. But later on I wasn't so sure.

I will now let you in on a professional secret. The very best place from which to cover a war is some reasonably comfortable city rather a long way from the front, particularly the kind of war that was now taking place in Blemi. The popular idea of going off into a bush with an armed column to watch the Sten guns and mortars at work, and

[53]

report the horrid little grapplings with the bullets flying all around is just amateurish. All those futile little slaughters don't decide a thing really. Who owns this little hill or that particular plantation or the other expanse of gray mud and saw grass doesn't matter at all. Even body counts don't matter because, as we all learned in Vietnam, there is an unlimited supply of bodies to count.

What does matter is who has got what road or bridge, or railroad, because cities and other points of government are absolutely at the mercy of roads, bridges and railroads. You get *that* news far more readily from the competent authorities in a nice clean city far removed from the front. Actually, at the front it is all confusion and nobody knows for sure who has got what. I remember in Korea attacking a village three times out of sheer nerves before we discovered that we'd been in possession of it for several hours. Also, at the front, even if you do get something solid, there's no way to get the news out in a hurry.

So I covered all the Blemi stuff from Mombasa and while it is very true that Zanzibar is much nearer and Dar es Salaam nearer still, neither has the Jesus fort or the Shamrock Club or Mrs. Blair's cooking—not to speak of the steady flow of news and goods coming out of Kenya. And then there was Major Anano. I once asked him outright whether he didn't think I could do a better job in Zanzibar. His huge white face went pink he was so shocked, and I felt sorry for him. In return he decided to do something really splendid for the Foreign Office.

"You ought to see Canon Kronk," he said. "He can put you on to a thought or two—a few things that someone in my position can't say at all."

"Changes in Catholic liturgy aren't news anymore," I said. "And in any case they are rather out of my line."

"Nothing to do with that at all, old man," said Anano. "Thought you might like to put your ear to the ground—in a new spot."

So I saw Canon Kronk at the Cathedral. He was a Czechoslovakian and he spoke English in a thick, muddy way which gave the impression that he had a thick, muddy mind. He had a large, round head set on what I can best describe as a large, round body and his neck was so short it was scarcely noticeable. His head was completely bald. To protect it from the sun, he wore a black beret, and that jaunty headpiece looked completely out of place on a man of his years. He was an inveterate cigarette smoker and rolled his own. He always had a little paper of cigarette in the corner of his mouth—a squeezed-up, wet, disgusting article with a little core of black tobacco in the middle. I suppose it would be more accurate to say that he sucked cigarettes rather than smoked them.

"Meesterrrr Weatherrrrs," he said. "Ourr new experrrt on East Afrrrican Affairrs. So glad to see you." That is the last sample I will give you of his accent. For the rest, you must imagine it yourself—the rolled *r*'s, the explosive *p*'s and *b*'s and *t*'s during which it was at times advisable to duck, each word coming out with a great deal of movement of his mouth, as if he had to pick the word from between his teeth and spit it out through his lips.

I ignored the sally and said I had dropped by to make his better acquaintance (I scarcely knew him) and asked whether he had heard anything from Father Felix and the nuns under his care at the Sacred Heart Mission.

"The sisters, thanks to our friends the British, are all safe," he said. "They were able to get to Tanganyika and they have been flown to Nairobi and they will be here in Mombasa tomorrow."

[55]

"Were they in danger?" I asked. "Was the mission threatened?"

"It is a prime target for Draki," said the Canon, and he took the little stub of cigarette out of the corner of his mouth between thumb and forefinger, examined it and put it back again. "The pagan forces are making a sweep in that direction. The mission is in essence what they intend to destroy. After all, they worship a drum. Don't forget that. If the sisters were captured—well, I need not describe to you what would happen to them. We are very grateful to the British."

"The nuns will be here tomorrow then?"

"Yes."

"There will be a press conference?"

"They will make a statement. No more. After all, these are people who have withdrawn from the world to serve God."

"Have you a copy of that statement they are going to make?" I asked.

He gave me an appreciative smile. "Ah, you American journalists," he said. "Such cynics. No. Reverend Mother will draw up her own statement (with which I will assist) and read it on behalf of the sisters?"

"And what about Father Felix?"

"He is not coming."

I thought of the banners of the Immaculate Conception and the Sacred Heart, and the approach of the pagan forces of Draki. "That figures," I said. "It's his mission."

Canon Kronk was annoyed. "No. It is not his mission," he exploded. "It is a mission of the Catholic Church. You have unwittingly put your finger on a sensitive point, my friend. That is the attachment of the blacks and people generally to a particular priest so that that person, rather than the divinity he serves, becomes the object of their affection and trust. A problem. A very big problem. It has existed all through our history—it will continue to the end of time."

"Cheer up, Canon," I said. "The Communists had the same problem under Stalin. The personality cult."

He removed his little wet piece of cigarette and spat on the terrace on which our conversation took place. "Communism means Mass Man—that's why *they* oppose the personality cult," he said. "The Church opposes Mass Man, preserves individual man, but must insure that devotion to any individual does not lead anyone away from God. A saint or a powerful figure is not a substitute for God, you know. Not that I would accuse Father Felix of anything but a true Christian devotion. But fifty years in one mission—you yourself said *his* mission, whereas it is a mission of the Church. You understand the situation."

"No," I said. "I don't understand it. But it doesn't really matter. Am I to conclude, however, that Father Felix was ordered to leave the mission with the nuns and refused to do so?"

"Father Felix was given the opportunity to leave with the sisters. He declined and decided to stay."

"Canon," I said, "I need a direct answer. Did you order him to leave?"

He was suddenly angry. He took the little butt of cigarette out of the corner of his mouth and threw it on the terrace and ground it to shreds under his boot. "Thunders, no," he said. "I did not order him to leave. I did not order him to leave for a very good reason—nobody gives orders to Father Felix. I told him to send away the

[57]

sisters and send away his parishioners and come himself to safety. He did what I told him to do, but elected to remain alone at the mission."

"So he will certainly be captured and probably killed," I said.

"Killed?" cried Canon Kronk, suddenly beside himself. "When Draki's men get there they'll do more than kill him. Remember, he is the archenemy—they'll flay him to death, or behead him or crucify him." He plunged on but I really didn't pay much attention, because in East Africa people are a little unbalanced when they talk about what will happen if the blacks ever get power. To head him off I suggested that Utori might decide to defend the mission, sending some forces to protect Father Felix, who after all was a well-known figure.

"Utori?" cried Canon Kronk. "That smiling, gutless product of a thatched hut and the University of Coimbra will not send a man to protect the mission. He says that Father Felix had every chance of evacuation and if he elected martyrdom instead he cannot save him from it. He says that Draki's thrust toward the mission in any case is only an attempt to divert him from securing Thompson's Crossing and driving into Draki's territory. He says he cannot get financial backing to save an old priest and his mission. Bankers need something more than that. They are not, after all, members of Alfred's Round Table." He meant Arthur's, of course.

"The Church has influence," I pointed out. "No doubt it is being used."

"If you think that the Church can rush off and save the life of every missionary who is in danger," he said snappishly, "you completely mistake her mission on earth. Her mission is to save souls—to preach the doctrine of Christ throughout the world. The Church can do nothing for him—nothing. Nothing at all."

I began to understand Anano's ploy now, of course. I was to do a piece about the fine old priest staying loyally with his mission, while the pagan forces of Draki, reeking of black magic, sin and darkness, poured down toward him, to engulf him and torture him to death. People react instantly to outrage. The whole of the United States would, in a week, be anti-Draki and pro-Utori, suiting the policy of the British Foreign Office as interpreted by Major Anano.

The only trouble was that this was my fourth or fifth war—World War II, Korea, Vietnam in its early stages and some of the now-forgotten war by the British against the Communists in Malaya, in which the Fijians, imported as trackers, did excellent work. When you've covered that many wars, atrocity stories and heroic stands begin to pall. Furthermore, I felt that either Canon Kronk was holding something back about Father Felix and his stand, or that thick, muddy mind of his had failed to appreciate some essential point concerning it.

Chapter Seven

I DIDN'T attend the press conference of the nuns, and it was just as well. They issued a completely colorless statement, rather fulsome in its praise of the British government and containing pious hopes for the survival of the Christian blacks who might find themselves in Draki's territory. It was a bad statement, propagandistic, full of generalities and lacking facts. In preparing it Canon Kronk had fallen into the error of imagining himself in the pulpit addressing the faithful, who were under a Christian obligation to believe what he said. On the subject of Father Felix, the statement was equally colorless. It said he had elected to remain behind at the mission but did not go into his motives or say what he hoped to do there.

Canon Kronk was annoyed that I had not attended the press conference. I explained to him that I was not a news reporter—that the kind of articles I wrote could not depend on a single news item, such as the return of the nuns, but had to go deeper into events. News, I pointed out, has no lasting value. It is mere gossip, exciting for perhaps one day, but of no use whatever the next. If he wanted something of lasting value about the mission and the nuns, then I would have to interview them at length.

To my surprise, my request for an interview was granted and I was given a private talk with Sister Elizabeth of the Cross, a thin, tall, sinewy woman of middle years, whose eyes were curiously wise and innocent at the same time. We sat at a table in a parlor at the rectory, if that is the word, attached to the Cathedral, and there was another, nameless sister present, seated on a chair away from the table and with her back to the wall. I felt a little flattered at this for after all I was getting on and it was nice to be thought of, seemingly, as a potential male menace.

Canon Kronk was not present physically, but he had plainly had a good talk to Sister Elizabeth of the Cross on the subject of discretion with the press, because for some time she merely talked around my questions.

"There were thirty-five children at the mission school," she said. "They have been sent back to the villages they came from. There are none left—none left at all. Some of the people have left the villages with the children and gone to Maikap. They are Blemis, you know—old enemies of the Bantu. By now, I suppose, most of the villages are empty. Wouldn't you say they are mostly empty, Sister?" And Sister, over by the wall, who was knitting a sock, agreed that they were.

"So the natural affection he feels for the mission which

he founded is the only reason Father Felix has decided to remain behind?" I asked.

"Yes," replied Sister Elizabeth, a little tightly, I thought.

"Sister," I said, "you seem to me to be holding something back. Is there really another reason? If a man is going to risk death for something, surely he is entitled at least to a guarantee that his motives should be thoroughly understood. Even if he's taken vows of obedience to his superiors, he has that right, hasn't he?"

The two sisters exchanged glances and Sister Elizabeth said, with some resolve, "I'm not sure that I can explain his real motives. He says, over and over again, 'The world has to make a stand. I have to give them a chance.' He's old. His mind is . . . unsound. He has it in his head that the whole world is going to drop whatever it is doing and rush to rescue the mission that he founded fifty years ago. There is no sense talking to him of all the things that have been destroyed in the Second World War and since then—our Order alone lost three convents and forty-three sisters. That merely confirms him in his view.

" 'You see,' he says, 'it is just as I have said. The world has to make a stand. I have to give it a chance.' And so he is there, all alone, and the world will do nothing for him." To my horror, she started to cry.

"I'm sorry," she said when she got command of herself. "I know his mission isn't that important and nobody will do anything for him. But he insists he is not doing this primarily to save the mission. He says it is much bigger than that. He believes that unless the world makes a stand now it is hopelessly lost. He's quite unconcerned. He really thinks that when the world knows his motives, it will step in to save him. Nothing will change his mind."

[63]

She was silent and I mulled over the outrageous challenge which the old priest with the solar topee and the Gladstone bag and the banners of the Sacred Heart had flung down to the whole of humanity. It numbed me, and while I was trying to recover my sense of proportion, Sister Elizabeth of the Cross looked across the table at me and said, very earnestly, "Mr. Weathers, he is all alone. Will you help him?"

And there it was—the direct personal appeal. Oh, I'd had them before, and occasionally in a good cause I've been able to pull a wire or two, provided nothing too troublesome was involved. But I'd never had such an appeal before from a seventy-year-old man pledging his life in an effort, as he saw it, to give the world a chance to recover its conscience. Right at that moment I believed that that was exactly what he was trying to do and, scarcely aware of what I was saying, I said, "Yes. I'll help him."

So, having turned down an offer from Utori to handle his press relations, I became an unsalaried press officer for Sister Elizabeth of the Cross and Father Felix. I wrote an article for *The New York Times* about Father Felix's position and they liked the angle that he was trying to give the world a chance to recover its conscience. In fact they ran an editorial saying that there were perhaps values other than Communism versus Capitalism with which the world should concern itself, and whatever the variety of individual beliefs or lack of them, the old priest remaining in his mission in one of the most backward parts of Africa was an example to mankind.

I gave the article and editorial to Sister Elizabeth, and the next day Mrs. Blair presented me with a small parcel, brought by a messenger, containing a pair of white knitted socks, so it is perhaps not quite true to say that I was unsalaried.

I called another press conference for Sister Elizabeth, and since I had persuaded Canon Kronk not to insist on a prepared statement, it was a much greater success than the first, which had been concerned with the sisters' travels by plane from Blemi to Mombasa. Newspapermen like an angle on a story. That's the whole secret of press-relations work. News is not a salable commodity without an angle, and the angle had better not be just propaganda. Sister Elizabeth, left to herself, was excellent. She stood up to the cameras and the lights and the microphones and gave the story with conviction and dignity. That's the great thing about a story, anyway—if you don't believe it yourself, nobody else ever will. And she believed it.

The angle was not that Father Felix was likely to be killed. It was that he was risking being killed to give the world a chance to recover its sense of values.

For a while it seemed as though Father Felix was going to win. There was tremendous publicity over the whole issue. A resolution was presented to the General Assembly of the United Nations calling for support of that body for the priest. It didn't pass because some were determined to identify Father Felix with Western Colonialism. But the debate and the publicity were in his favor. A statement supporting the priest was read into the *Congressional Record* by a congressman who was also a Presbyterian clergyman, and for a while there was perhaps as much concern over the fate of Father Felix as there had once been about the fate of Livingstone, the prototype with which he had become identified.

But then there came, as is always the case, the counter-

[65]

attack. It was far more vigorous than I had anticipated and it concentrated on a point on which Father Felix was particularly vulnerable—population control.

You will recall how Father Felix, at our meeting in the Shamrock Club, had made that astonishing and utterly unprovoked statement about infant mortality being lower in his district of Blemi than in New York City if you counted abortions? Well, I wasn't the only person to whom he had made such statements. It turned out that he had corresponded vigorously with antiabortion and anticontraceptive movements in many countries and was completely rabid on the subject of population control. Then somebody turned up the fact that for all his years of preaching Christianity, there never had been a black nun or a black priest at his mission, and his attitude toward the blacks was said to be that they were not really the same as whites. (I remember that years ago something of the same charge was leveled against Schweitzer at Lambarene.) In short, Father Felix was labeled a racial bigot and a foolish old man, the product of an outdated religion linked with repressive colonialism. If he was killed he had nobody to blame but himself.

Draki, on the other hand, began to emerge as a sort of Messiah of the Bantu. He became a spiritual and national leader of a people long oppressed and denied their religious and cultural rights. He began to look like Haile Selassie, the Lion of Judah, only a little larger; and that story of his being imprisoned for eating a three-year-old child was condemned as an example of the British using their colonial law system to blacken the reputation of potential public figures.

Canon Kronk, when all this reaction broke out, was almost grimly triumphant. "You see," he said. "You see what happens when one sets himself up to challenge the world? The whole Church suffers for the personality of an individual. Do you see now why I didn't want to make a big issue of Father Felix? What was to be expected? Vilification. That is all. Vilification."

"Canon," I said, "it is true that Father Felix is somewhat rabid on the subject of abortion. But his views on that subject and the subject of birth control exactly match the views of your church."

He was furious. "Bah," he exploded. "You people never listen. The Church has supported birth control long before it ever became a public issue. But we support natural birth control," and he went off into a tirade about chemistry being no substitute for character to which I paid no attention. Only one phrase struck home. "We must be on the side of life," he said. "There is no alternative."

There was no denying at all that the counterattack against Father Felix was effective. It shook my own sympathy for him. I asked myself whether what he meant about the conscience of mankind might not be, after all, some high-sounding phrase to cover his antiquated views on population control. And then there was the matter of the absence of black nuns or priests at his mission, which embodied his whole attitude, as I saw it, toward blacks.

I took that question up with Sister Elizabeth of the Cross, and she said that it was quite true that there had never been any black nuns or priests at the mission.

"But that's because the people won't listen to a priest who comes from among themselves," she added.

"Which makes Christianity a white man's religion, a religion adhered to by blacks only because it is preached by the technologically superior whites," I said.

She considered that statement for a while and then said,

"No. I know you are not a religious man, Mr. Weathers. But if you were, would you confess your sins to someone who had been your playmate at school, or listen to sermons from someone you had grown up with? It's an involved problem, but it isn't because they are black that we don't have black nuns at the mission. It's because they're local."

"I'm sorry, Sister," I said. "That just won't wash. There are surely black nuns from other parts who could have served at the mission. None ever did."

"There certainly are," she said. "My Superior, Reverend Mother Mary Martha, is black. But we don't use black nuns to prove that we are not racist. We use them to serve God." It was quite a rebuke.

When I complained of Father Felix's outspoken and unprovoked views on abortion and kindred subjects she said calmly, "What other view could he take? We can't just take a fashionable point of view."

"Population control isn't just a fad," I said. "The statistics show without any quibble whatever that if world population continues to grow at the present rate, there just will not be room or substance for people to live a decent human life. We will be crowded together like rats in a cage. That isn't speculation or fashion or hysteria, but plain statistical fact."

I was annoyed. I had stuck my neck out with that article in *The New York Times*. Father Felix, I had said, was offering his life to give the world a chance to recover its conscience. And there was room to argue now that Father Felix actually represented white paternalism and an almost hysterical stand against birth control.

When we parted, Sister Elizabeth said, "I'm sorry that you feel as you do, Mr. Weathers. I hope we part friends."

I said, somewhat coldly, that we did, and she went off
with the other nun, her habit flowing around her, like a
figure from the Middle Ages, going back through the
centuries to where she rightly belonged.

Chapter
Eight

THAT is the place to which I consigned the two of them for a while—the Middle Ages. They were misguided and they suffered from a "culture lag." It is surprising how comforting to injured pride an apt term is.

At this point the cause of Father Felix was at its lowest ebb. It was entirely his own fault. He had been so outspoken on his favorite subject, so lacking in discretion or prudence or even reasonableness, that all other aspects of his work were lost and for a while it seemed that everybody believed he had elected to remain at his mission not as a priest faithful to his life's work but as a bigot determined to focus the attention of the world on what he had described in one now-famous letter as "the war on motherhood."

My own feelings about him were ambiguous. My pride

was involved. I felt that, as a professional journalist, I had been lured into a trap by a weeping nun with wise but innocent eyes. Of course, I didn't believe that Father Felix was entirely motivated by the cause on which he had been so outspoken in his correspondence. I sensed there was something more than that in his decision. But I felt that the sisters had been less than frank with me, for apart from his surprising outburst at our first meeting, this aspect of Father Felix was entirely new to me. The cause was sullied and I decided to withdraw from the field, as it were, and have nothing more to do with him.

Meanwhile the war in Blemi sputtered on. The main thrust of Draki's Bantu forces was toward Thompson's Crossing, to the north—a key point on the Blemi river held, or rumored to be held, by Utori's Republicans. The Sacred Heart Mission lay about a hundred and fifty miles to the south, but on Draki's side of the river. A force of unknown size was reported moving toward it under the command of an Alsatian mercenary called Schwartz. Skinner had never mentioned Schwartz to me, but Anano knew him.

"Nasty piece of work," he said. "But a first-class soldier. An expert. You have to admire him. He fights for whatever side provides the highest pay. That side happens to be Draki's right now."

"Where does Draki get his money?" I asked.

"If Moscow won't do, I haven't got an answer," said Anano.

A little later, while the counterattack on Father Felix still raged, I got a cable from Utori. It read:

"Your angle on Father Felix impressive. Am sending a column to his relief and offer you exclusive, repeat exclusive, coverage, with full uncensored facilities. Reply immediately. Sincere admiration and congratulations. Utori."

I replied, declining the offer and saying that it appeared that Father Felix was not simon-pure and might be merely a propagandist for antiabortion laws.

The following day Utori replied:

"Always admired your frankness but for my purposes Father Felix remains the conscience of mankind. Take Mombasa Airlines to Nairobi where Colonel Selim BRA" —that meant Blemi Republican Army—"will fly you to Maikap. Delay may be fatal to Father Felix. This I admit is coercion, but bribery has already failed in your case. Utori."

There wasn't any need to show the cable to Anano because he knew of it already and so did half of Mombasa. I have to say for Anano that he ran true to form and applied his own particular brand of arm-twisting to get me to accept Utori's offer.

"Bloody risky business all around," he said. "No protection for you at all—not like in a decent army. Oh, Utori wouldn't do you any harm, of course. But those mercenaries are frightful beasts. No military code of conduct at all. And as for their troops—well, you'd be just as well off among headhunters. I wouldn't blame you if you turned the whole thing down. Confidentially, Holmes of the *Manchester Guardian* has been after me, asking me to use what little influence I may have to get him to Maikap in your stead. I told him that I haven't got any influence."

The big surprise was a cable from *The New York Times.* I never found out whether this originated with the British (which would be Anano to the British Resident Commissioner in Zanzibar to the Colonial Office in London to the Foreign Office to the British Ambassador in

Washington to *The New York Times* Editor) or Utori (direct cable to the *Times* with details of his exclusive offer to me) or was even perhaps the work of the Sister Elizabeth-Canon Kronk-Vatican axis. The cable said, in part:

"We must urge you to accompany the Father Felix relief column as our editorial position has been challenged and the fullest personal report of the facts is essential to our reputation. Interview with Felix at mission besides being magnificent journalistic achievement of Pulitzer standard vital now. Barclays Nairobi instructed to meet every expense. Good luck. Coulter."

The cable, on reflection, left me very little choice in the matter. Not to go meant that I could forget about selling anything further to *The New York Times* for quite a while, and no journalist in my position could afford to lose that market. Then, Father Felix was my story. I had rightly or wrongly brought him onto the world stage, and I couldn't just cop out and leave him there, much as I would have liked to. So in the end I decided I had to go and booked my plane passage and cabled Utori and the *Times*.

It was nice to know that I could draw on the Barclays Bank in Nairobi for expenses, charging *The New York Times* account, and I decided viciously that since I had to go I would have a thousand dollars out of their hide for starters. I dropped in at the Shamrock Club for a last drink before taking off—I hate flying—and Robinson, the Scottish doctor with the obscene, indeed blasphemous mind, came charging over to shake my hand. "Yir a guid man, Weathers," he said. "A guid man. If ye ever hae the pox, there'll be no fee." But what really gave me food for thought was a glimpse of Sister Elizabeth with her companion nun at the airport when I took off.

A Robinson-Sister Elizabeth of the Cross-Anano axis? Well, I was feeling a little light-headed.

Colonel Selim turned out to be, not a Moslem, as I had anticipated, but a Sikh and a former officer of the British Army in India. He'd retired on pension after the Partition of India (partition is Britain's speciality) and tried his hand at farming in Kenya, but the pastoral life he found was not for him. So he'd offered his services to Utori as a mercenary and now was a military adviser of sorts but, more important, Utori's personal pilot. His beard had gray in it so I suppose he was in his mid-fifties. He was a very good flier and a quiet, handsome man, neat and clean, with a vast amount of discretion. He and his plane were entirely at my disposal and he had reserved rooms for me, if required, at the Royal African (British) or the Nairobi Hilton (American). My choice.

The rooms were reserved under his name, as he thought I might want to avoid publicity. That didn't work, however. The only place you can secure anonymity is in a city and Nairobi, although a city, is also part of that huge African village. So I had to give an interview to local newsmen (it's a curious thing for one newspaperman to be interviewed by another newspaperman) but I declined to talk on local television. Nairobi all in all was behind Father Felix.

For one thing he was a white man, and in Africa all white men are kin. For another, Nairobi was conservative—British rather than mod-British—and public opinion on the whole was opposed to abortion, except in the case of rape by blacks. If a third argument was required it would be that Father Felix was a famous figure in all East Africa. You always cheer for your own when attacked by outsiders.

We stayed two days in Nairobi. I sensed that Colonel

Selim wanted to leave for Maikap as soon as possible, but I felt that I had been to a large degree trapped by Utori or by Major Anano or by Sister Elizabeth or a combination of all three into going, and I was in no hurry. When Colonel Selim hinted that the relief column was waiting for me, I replied that it could leave without me, for I was sure I could catch it before it arrived at the mission. He replied, calmly, patiently, that it would not leave until I arrived.

"Why not?" I asked.

"Mr. Weather," replied the Colonel, "it is a matter, I suspect, of propaganda. But isn't that your field?"

"No," I said. "My field is truth. There is a difference between truth and propaganda."

He smiled, a polite, civilized, patient smile. "The problem of truth puzzled even Pilate," he said.

During the two days I spent with him in Nairobi, he never volunteered any information, but he answered all my questions quietly and efficiently. The Republican troops had control over the greater part of Blemi except for the hill area in the northeast, where Draki's Royalists ruled. The problem was that this was a "bush" war, and even if all the cities were taken by the Republicans, there was still the huge problem of subduing the "bush" countryside. There were several large pro-Draki pockets even in the Republican area, and many tribes and villagers who were not pro-Draki were afraid to come out against him and his followers, and supported them when they were in their neighborhood.

"Fear is a terrible weapon, as you know," said Colonel Selim. "A row of heads on stakes, along the roadside, reeking and covered with flies, will keep a whole area trembling."

"Propaganda," I said. "Atrocity stories don't impress me. It is very simple to cut off the heads of a few men killed in some bush fight, put them on stakes, photograph them and point to an atrocity by the opposing side."

"Mr. Weathers," said the Colonel, "believe me, I would never even have thought of that. You have a gift in that area."

We left for Maikap one morning just before dawn. Only the top of Kilimanjaro, snow-clad the year round, burned gold in the dark sky as we took off. Colonel Selim advised an early start to avoid the heavy thermals of midday and he was right because, even so, in that light jet we were flung kitelike hundreds of feet up in the air and then dropped like a stone hundreds of feet down again, so that I spent a lot of the journey absolutely terrified, and at one time reached for the oxygen mask over my head, for it seemed to me that the cabin had lost pressure and I could not breathe.

We soared out of the pool of darkness over the earth and up into the blinding sunlight, and then hurtled our way across swamp and desert and forest and foothill, with but one glimpse of a road, and that a track, until we came suddenly to Maikap—a little huddle of corrugated-iron roofs and a tired square around which stood some lumpish adobe buildings. We had to circle the airstrip twice while tiny figures below got two water buffalo off the runway. When we were down and had taxied to a stop, Colonel Selim turned to me and said, "Mr. Weathers, I think that, for you, the worst part of the journey is over. You are not a flier by nature."

"Colonel," I said, "if you have anything to do with getting me out of this damned country, for God's sake send me by road."

Chapter Nine

UTORI was delighted at my arrival. He wasn't at the air-strip to meet me, but he had sent his Minister of the Interior, a thin, thoughtful Portuguese whose long bony face and straggly beard reminded me of a painting I had seen once of St. Jerome, I think, by El Greco. It is curious to note, in passing, how Spanish concepts of holiness are always embodied in misery and emaciation. This gentleman, Senhor Martin Lacerda to anglicize his name a little, embraced me piously and conducted me to a beautiful large Daimler sedan into which I was swept and then driven half a mile to the Presidential Palace, where Utori awaited me.

"Ah, Mr. Weathers," said Utori, beaming and open as usual. "You see we are intended to work together, you and I. I knew it the moment we met. Everything is going swimmingly. We have been able to push the Royalists away from Thompson's Crossing—I have the radio message here—and the column we are sending to defend the conscience of mankind is ready to move out in the morning. Captain Prescott will be in command. You must meet him immediately."

He spoke into one of a nest of telephones on his desk (two of them, I noted, were not even connected), and in came Captain Prescott, a tall, lean Englishman, very military in appearance, with a close-clipped moustache, sparse hair brushed stiffly back and a black patch over one eye. I am old enough to remember the advertisements for Hathaway shirts and at the sight of the black patch I almost burst out laughing.

Captain Prescott was in "mufti," as he put it later. He was wearing a pair of beautifully pressed gray flannel slacks and a blue blazer, with the embroidered crest of some school, university or perhaps regiment on the pocket. I disliked him immediately. I am well aware that such first impressions are generally held to be unreliable, but I have rarely found that to be the case. It seemed to me that Captain Prescott had summoned to his aid all the props of officer and gentleman, thereby demonstrating that he was neither an officer nor a gentleman. I also got the impression that Utori was aware of my reaction and interested, rather than dismayed.

Captain Prescott shook my hand and said he was glad to have me along on the "show," that we would be moving off at dawn and he would have a man "knock me up" with a cup of tea at four. "Anything I can do for you, let me know," he said and then, with a glance at Utori, "There are one or two things I ought to take care of personally. . . ."

"Certainly," said Utori and dismissed him. When he was gone he said, "He'll be utterly drunk by midnight, roaring around from bar to bar (we have perhaps a dozen in Maikap) in bush clothes with hand grenades dangling from his shirt, singing, swearing, fighting, drinking, chasing women. But he will still have those officer and gentleman clothes of his carefully folded and put away somewhere—for when he's an officer and gentleman again. Were you ever in England?"

I said no. I knew only such Englishmen as I had met abroad.

"Well, in England, every Englishman of the middle and lower classes has a dream. It consists, I think, of wearing clothes like Captain Prescott's, but wearing them as to the manner born, and taking part in tennis games with beautiful ladies at weekend parties at manor houses, or perhaps punting gracefully down the Thames and talking wittily of Mozart and cricket. Do Americans have such a dream, Mr. Weathers?"

"The American dream starts with a dollar bill and goes on from there until there are enough of them to buy the country houses, the punts and the beautiful ladies," I said. I was feeling malicious.

"Very practical," said Utori. "I like that better. Now about Father Felix. We understand each other perfectly, I am sure. I was mistaken about him in the beginning and nearly blundered. In fact I did blunder. I said that he had elected martyrdom though offered every chance of saving himself, and I didn't see how I was going to get the money and support I needed to establish the Republic by defending him. Actually I was right. What money and support I have received and will receive are properly on a quid pro quo basis—mining rights, forestry rights, rail-

[81]

road contracts—these are the securities needed to get money and political support. But they have to be dressed in terms of human values. And the freeing of the people of Blemi from the dead hand of Portuguese colonialism just isn't enough. It sounds like propaganda. It has a kind of—well—Communist ring. Nonetheless, it is true. I assure you it is true. I loved the Portuguese, as I told you in Mombasa, until I came to realize that they were never going to allow us blacks to be full human beings—human beings of the first rate, not the third rate.

"And then you put everything in a human frame for me—magnificently. What was the phrase? 'To give the world a chance to recover its conscience.' Beautiful. Mr. Weathers—may I call you Michael?—Michael, you have a talent for propaganda which is unique. Certainly the Republic of Blemi must rise to that occasion—must be the first of all the nations of the world to go to the defense of the Conscience of the World. That being so, who will not support us—who will declare himself our enemy? My dear Michael—yes, I am going to call you Michael—when I read your splendid article in *The New York Times,* I wept. Yes. Wept for joy, and I look on you as a—well—a gift from God. The Conscience of Mankind. And all I could come up with was 'the dead hand of Portuguese colonialism.' "

He pulled open the center drawer of his desk and threw a folder containing a sheaf of papers on his desk. "Look at these," he said. "Cables of congratulation, of support, of praise from groups in every country in the world. The National Council of Churches in America, the National Conference of Christians and Jews, the Archbishop of Canterbury, the Patriarch of the Greek Orthodox community, there's even one in there from the Copts in Abys-

[82]

sinia. Here, read them yourself." He thrust the cablegrams at me and I noted that quite a number were addressed to me.

"Look," I said, "the phrase about giving the world a chance to recover its conscience is mine. I'll admit that. But you surely know now that there are other aspects of Father Felix with which much of the world disagrees—quite rightly, in my view. You ought to go into this thing with your eyes open."

"My dear Michael," said Utori, "what does it matter? It is too bad that his views on abortion came out, but that can surely be remedied with a few more articles by yourself. And, in any case, are you really being fair to the good Father Felix? Maybe he is being misquoted by his enemies."

"His enemies don't have to misquote him," I said. "All they have to do is quote him correctly."

Utori shook his head. "Up to a point, a very minor point, men shape events," he said. "Then the events seize the men and fling them down the road of history like leaves caught in a hurricane. We have arrived at that point, you and I, Michael. If I were now not to lift my hand to defend the Conscience of the World, my whole cause would be ruined. I would be held as callous, as anti-white, as anti-Christian as Draki. No. I have to defend him."

"He is not necessarily the Conscience of the World," I said, irritated.

"You must learn to look on the bright side, as I do," said Utori. "You must learn to see what profit can be made out of any set of circumstances. I was always an optimist, you know. I even trusted the Portuguese and believed in them. And this is just what I was looking for to put our whole revolution into focus. We stand for the

Conscience of Mankind. We are going to the rescue of Father Felix." He rose, putting his arm around my shoulder, walked with me out of the room and down a wide corridor with overhead vast fans being slowly moved by what seemed to me tired electricity. Somewhere nearby I could hear the drumming of a generator.

"Here is your office," he said, opening a door. "On that telephone you can reach *The New York Times*. Mr. Coulter's extension number is three-five-seven in case you haven't got that little detail. You will perhaps want to telephone a story about the success of our forces at Thompson's Crossing and about your own start tomorrow morning. Don't worry about the bill. We'll take care of that. In return, of course, we will listen in to your telephone conversation, but nothing in life is free, dear boy.

"On your desk you will find a press release giving the details of our victory at Thompson's Crossing. It is true that we are now in firm command of the crossing, but it is not at all true that our side is ready and anxious for a thrust deep into Draki's territory. Actually, we have lost about thirty per cent from desertion. And we didn't take the stronghold in a fierce hand-to-hand encounter as the release says. We burned it out with napalm first and machine-gunned the Bantu as they came out. You see, I hold nothing back from you."

"You sound as though you enjoy it," I said.

"I don't now, but it is possible that I will someday," Utori replied. "What is power, after all, if it isn't the power to kill? Nothing but a shadow. Don't look so shocked. You've never had that power. Wait until you do. There are some pictures with the press releases, but they'd have to go by air to Nairobi. I send a plane once a day."

The pictures were unpublishable—a mound of human

hands and feet with a couple of dogs sniffing at it and one of a huge crucifix with two women hanging, one from each arm. One of them had a baby strapped to her. I tore the filthy things up because there is a time in life when a man is entitled to turn away from such things.

There was a good electric typewriter on the desk, but the tired electricity that moved the tired fans in the corridor seemed incapable of operating it. The typewriter whirred and worked in spasms and fell quiet, so I wrote a reasonable account of the Thompson's Crossing victory in longhand to send on the plane, incorporating in it the story of my arrival in Maikap and plans for departure to Father Felix's mission. I certainly wasn't going to call New York and telephone the story, so I was surprised when the telephone rang and a voice said, "Mr. Weathers? New York calling. Please hold the line."

Then, a moment later: "This is Tom Coulter of the *Times,* Mr. Weathers. I heard you'd been trying to get me."

"No, I haven't," I said. "But it seems that Utori wants me to try to get you. Well, since you're on the line maybe I can give you a story." So I gave him the Thompson Crossing details and the story about my own departure.

"We need a detailed interview with Father Felix in which he sets out his viewpoint and his reason for taking his stand," said Coulter when I had finished. "I am delighted you are on your way. By the way, we have received a packet of pretty appalling atrocity pictures here . . ."

I sighed, an expensive trans-African, trans-Atlantic sigh. "I've just torn up the dupes," I said.

"Quite right," said Coulter. "We couldn't use them. Well. Good luck."

"Thanks," I said and hung up.

[*85*]

I dined with Colonel Selim at his house, and after dinner he drove me over to my bungalow, which was in the government residential quarter.

"You are not a fighting man, Mr. Weathers?" he said when we parted.

"No, Colonel, I am not," I replied. "The last fight I was in was at the Columbia-Harvard game in 'thirty-two. Somebody swiped my flask."

He smiled his gentle, dignified smile and, putting his hand in the pocket of his military tunic, drew out a small nickel-plated handgun. "It's best not to use a gun until you absolutely have to," he said. "But when you have to, do not hesitate."

"How do you know when you have to?" I countered.

"I am sure your judgment will be sound," he replied. "When you reached for the oxygen in the plane, we actually had lost pressure. Good night."

We shook hands. I liked Colonel Selim.

Chapter
Ten

THE reason that tank battles and engagements between armored cars and half-tracks are mostly inconclusive is that the assailants on both sides are seasick. That very obvious explanation only became apparent to me after the first two days of our journey, south and somewhat east, from Maikap to the Mission of the Sacred Heart on the eastward side of the Blemi river.

During the first day we traveled along reasonable roads. They would have been called very bad roads back home in the States and, I think, second-class roads in most of Europe. But they were reckoned good roads in Blemi and though they were full of potholes, this didn't impede the half-track in which I was riding. The roads petered out in midmorning of the following day and we bucketed and churned and swayed and lurched across the virgin bush—

a dry hell of stunted acacia, some kind of thornbush and clumps of stuff which I was assured was grass but looked like dried cornstalks to me. I think the name elsewhere is arrowweed.

One hour of this and I was appallingly seasick. I was not only seasick but I believed solemnly that I was going to stifle to death in the thick curtains of dust which the half-track ahead flung up into the air and from which we never seemed to be able to escape. My vehicle was driven by a huge black, Lieutenant Bomba. He was one of those men who are intended by God, by Nature, by biology or whatever is the creative force, to spend all their lives in the open and who are rendered uncomfortable in any kind of habitation. He was a massive man—huge shoulders, huge head, huge arms and hands, and buttocks like a bull. He was blacker than any other black man I have ever seen, a kind of plum-black, and when he opened his mouth to laugh (which he did very often) the explosion of white teeth and pink tongue in that black cannonball of a face was startling.

He was seasick too, but in the way that an animal is. After half an hour of bucketing he stopped the half-track and heaved copiously over the side. Then he spat, wiped his eyes, took a drink of water and went on. For him his sickness was vented in one monstrous expulsion, and after that he would turn around at me, collapsed and green, on the seat behind him, a seat to which I was fastened by webbing, and expose to me his huge pink-and-white grin in his enormous black face.

I came to think of him as the devil. I know that sounds farfetched. But if you were suffering from waves of nausea; if the only air you could breathe was heavy with dust and the stench of Diesel exhaust; if through this there struck a blinding sun; and if, your whole world filled with noise and lurching, a big black head was turned toward you every now and then and you were exposed to a vast pink-and-white grin, I think you would conclude that you were in the hands of the devil too.

Actually Bomba was a good guy. He knew I was American and he had served under an American NCO called Colby—Sergeant Colby—in the Spanish Army in Morocco. Yes, he was a mercenary too. His home was in the Sudan. So, knowing I was American, he consoled me occasionally with the one phrase he believed especially dear to my people. "Son of a bitch," he would say. "Son of a bitch." And through all my nausea for a whole day he gave me the only consolation he could offer—his pink-and-white grin accompanied by the expression "son of a bitch."

It was no consolation to me at all that Captain Prescott wasn't in the slightest degree sick. He should have had a hangover that would stagger a mule, but if so, he didn't show it. He had spent the night carousing in the bars of Maikap, but by the midafternoon of the first day had sobered up and had a dinner of pork and beans (Heinz) and the haunch of a small deer, hardly much bigger than a goat, which someone had shot out on that horrible bushland. I couldn't eat. I might have been tempted by a little chicken broth and some salt crackers, but pork and beans and greasy haunch of dubious venison was beyond me.

Captain Prescott was amused. There is a certain type of Englishman who delights in showing physical superiority to lesser breeds—eating when others can't, enduring cold when others are shivering, walking when any sensible man would wait for a ride. It is a surviving Teutonic quality in some of the English, who as a people like to deny any link with the Germans. Captain Prescott had that trait to a marked degree, and showed off by eating copiously while I lay on a camp cot, eyes closed, grateful for a little air and rendered queasy by the aroma from his plate of food. He ate from a plate, of course—with a knife and fork and, believe it or not, a napkin which he called a serviette. His dinner was laid out on a folding table and he sat on a folding campstool. The officer and gentleman had returned after the night on the town.

When, on the third day, I managed to join him for dinner—I was two days without eating—he didn't express any pleasure at my recovery but ate somewhat more copiously than necessary, pressed food on me and hinted that it was a mark of American weakness that my appetite was so poor.

"Fine man, Captain Prescott," said Bomba to me later. "First-class gentleman."

"Son of a bitch," I replied and was rewarded by that wonderful pink-and-white explosion.

Prescott took me up on this—he had overheard the remark, for he was not far away at the time. He took me aside and said, "Look here, Weathers, I don't know what the rules are in *your* country, but in *my* country it is considered very bad form to make derogatory remarks about an officer to his inferiors."

"Listen, Prescott," I said, "I don't know what your goddam country is, but how did you immediately know that when I said 'Son of a bitch' I was referring to you?"

"Of all the infernal nerve," he said. "I'd have you know that I'm the commanding officer here and you are part of my command."

"If you want to come out of this little jaunt a hero, Prescott," I said, "you'd better keep on my right side. I don't know whether you are a good soldier or the town drunk, but as far as the world is concerned, you are what I say you are and don't forget it." That gave him something to think about and, as matters turned out, it seems that he thought about it a great deal.

The next day, in any case, I got my own back on him. We came to an area of swamp and sedges over which the half-tracks could not go. There we parted company with them. They left to return to Maikap and we had to carry on our own backs the Stens and BARs and all the ammunition and food and even a water-cooled Vickers machine gun—a weapon which I doubt has been used anywhere in the world this side of World War II. The Vickers was Prescott's pet, though two men had to struggle with it hour after hour slung from poles on their shoulders. Lieutenant Bomba carried the tripod as if it were a twig and a belt of .303 ammunition swathed around him without the slightest trace of tiring. He seemed to gain energy from the sun, which, as it were, recharged his batteries, and it gave me a great deal of comfort to see those massive shoulders ahead and those tough buttocks rolling powerfully under the ammo belt.

When we got to the swamp area—sedges, saw grass and little pools of water thick with green slime—Captain Prescott forgot about his superior hardiness and, letting others go ahead, dropped to the rear of his men. Bomba was ahead, then two others, then me, then the rest—thirty in all, with Prescott behind. I thought this a military disposition but discovered that the saw grass and the sedge and all the other entangled vegetable matter that we slipped and struggled through was infested with bloodsucking ticks and tiny leeches.

The leeches got up about as far as the groin, and the ticks came down to about the waist. They didn't invade each other's territory and there was a kind of no-man's-land from the navel to the groin which was comparatively free of either. Well then, for all his resistance to hangovers and seasickness, the reason that the hardy Captain Prescott took up the rear in going through the swamp was that he was scared almost to hysteria of the leeches and ticks. He let his own men go ahead as bait for them, so that he, coming behind, was scarcely touched. It seems that he had heard that you could get rabies from the leeches, which occasionally fastened on a rabid animal.

I amused myself at dinner that night asking whether there wasn't a leech on his knee or his wrist, and said that it was usual in my country for officers not to expose men to hazards from which they drew back themselves. He got so angry that he left the little camp table and his dinner and went off to sulk in his tent. After a while I felt a little sorry for him. It is a weakness of mine to feel sorry for phonies when they have been exposed. So I was kinder to him later, and later still I discovered that in the matter of soldiering, he wasn't a phony at all.

When we camped that night at the edge of a fearsome forest, beyond the saw grass swamp, the radiotelephone, powered by twelve-volt batteries, also carried slung between poles, would not work. Prescott fiddled gloomily with it for a long time. Nobody answered us, not even when he transmitted in Morse, which took less power. He kept up his hopeless fiddling while the men hung around anxiously, for that radiotelephone was a sort of security blanket for them. When they were quite convinced that it wouldn't work, and probably would never work again, one of them took a kerosene can, wrapped a blanket around it and, holding it between his knees, began tapping it in various parts with a stick.

"Bush telegraph," said Lieutenant Bomba. "Better than wireless." But the only result as far as I was concerned was that all through the night the fool kept banging on the muffled kerosene can, trying to make it "talk." If you can tolerate a digression, the method is very simple. First you decide on the dialect to be used—all through Blemi, Swahili was the international tongue, so the drummer used Swahili. The next problem was to fix the drum so that it was capable of making several different sounds within a range of, say, five half-tones. Once that was done, and the places to hit for each half-tone mastered, then a kind of Swahili speech could be sent on the drum by striking the appropriate half-tones in the correct rhythm. It can hardly be done with English, because English is spoken in a very flat manner, as is French. But Swahili and many other African tongues are replete with rising or falling tones, which have not been eroded down to fit into an alphabet. The next morning the boy who brought me my tea told me that the drum had talked very well, but there was nobody listening.

"Maybe they're listening and don't want to reply," I said.

"No, sir," he said, "everybody replies to the drum."

We had all spent a miserable night. The blacks minded the leeches somewhat more than I did, perhaps because they knew more about them. They built a fire and scooped up handfuls of wood ash and took an ash bath to rid themselves of them. I did the same, halfheartedly, but was so weary that after dinner I just collapsed on my camp cot and spent a nightmare night with the drum banging away, conscious that there were little creatures crawling about me. As soon as I had my tea in the morning, I stripped down and rubbed myself all over with cool wood ash and then wasted half a gallon of water by pouring it over my-self from a dipper. But it was well worth it. I felt as if I had grown a new, clean skin.

Then we went on out of the saw grass and into the forest. This had two advantages. The branches of the trees overhead interlocked so that sunlight hardly penetrated to the floor, which was knee-deep (and more) in places with black humus, so the interior of the forest was cool. Second, there were no ticks and leeches and very few mosquitoes. We sweated, of course—it wasn't that cool. Sweating so heavily, I grew appallingly thirsty and had to keep stopping for a drink of water. Prescott didn't take a drink from the time we broke camp to the end of the day. But he didn't rub it in. And at the end of the day he offered me a drink of whisky from his private stock. There was, then, peace between us.

"How much further?" I asked when I had accepted the drink.

"If the river we crossed yesterday is the Sinali, half a day more will see us there."

"You don't know?" I asked.

He shrugged. "One tree looks like another tree—one river horribly like another river. If the river was the Zueta, we've two more days to go."

"What about the men? Don't they know?"

He smiled. He didn't really smile, but he bared his teeth in my direction and then unbared them. It was the best he could do in the matter of smiling and he must have practiced it for hours.

"Mr. Weathers," he said, "the men are Africans. African blacks will tell you only what they think you want to hear. They don't like to give bad news. Ask any one of them and he will tell you that the river was the Sinali. Nobody will say the Zueta."

I asked, and they all said the Sinali except Bomba, who said that the river was a river.

"What about the drummer?" He'd been banging away during the evening again. "Has he had any reply?"

"Yes," said Prescott. "As a matter of fact, he has. He says that the others are behind us—two days."

"What others?" I asked, for I had forgotten.

"Draki's men," said Prescott. "Under Schwartz. He's a real bastard. Alsatian."

"What's that got to do with it?" I asked.

"Ask Bomba," was the reply.

And when I asked Bomba he gave me his pink-and-white grin and said, "Real son of a bitch, sir. Real son of a bitch."

Chapter
Eleven

THE river was the Sinali and at midmorning of the following day we came, to my huge surprise, upon a track through the forest which led down to the Blemi. There was a bridge, literally of poles and twisted vines, leading across the river; and when we had gone cautiously over this and mounted a bluff beyond, there before us lay the mission in its little clearing of fields, some of pasture and some tilled. In one of the pastures, peaceful and reassuring, browsed two cows, one white and the other a kind of gray-brown. There was a flag flying over the mission and Prescott examined it carefully through field glasses, said, "Well, I'll be damned" and handed the field glasses to me. It was the banner of the Sacred Heart—the great beef heart with the flames bursting out of the top of it.

"Well, he's still there," said Prescott, making the obvious remark. "Come on." And we walked through the fields and past the low mud walls of the mission and into the compound which they surrounded.

There was Father Felix, with his solar topee clapped on his head, feeding some hens with grain kept in a dirty enameled basin. Our meeting was a complete anticlimax. We staggered in loaded down with guns, ammunition belts, grenades, radiotelephone, batteries and God knows what, making a great military fuss and clatter, and Father Felix hardly looked up from the hens, the picture of rustic charm, but nodded and went on tossing out grain. We stood around him, taken aback, and then Lieutenant Bomba put down the tripod of the Vickers and stepped out of that vast serpent of ammunition which he had carried coiled about him for days. He reached out and took the basin of feed from the priest and, grinning his huge and startling grin, happily threw golden handfuls of grain to the hens.

Prescott was disappointing. His mind was formed for clichés. He said when he recovered himself, "Father Felix, I presume." Yes, that's what he said, instead of something like "Pardon me, but is this the road to Vladivostok?"

The priest looked at him gravely and replied with a touch of humor, "Yes, Father Felix. Livingstone is dead, you know."

"I'm Captain Howard Prescott, Blemi Republican Army, come to your relief, sir," he said. "I'm glad we got here in time. Schwartz is only a few hours behind us. We've got time to get out if we move fast."

"Get out?" cried Father Felix. "I have no intention of getting out. I'm staying here. I have to stay here. It is important to the whole world that I stay here."

"Look, Padre," said Prescott, "it's impossible to hold

this place. It's exposed from every side, and those walls—they're not even protection from rifle fire. Schwartz will have mortars—he loves them. We'll be overwhelmed."

"Then you'd better leave," said Father Felix. "I'm staying."

"But you can't expect me to put my men into such a trap and order them to stay," said Prescott.

"I don't know what to expect," said Father Felix gravely. "It isn't to save me that you've come here. I'm an old man and must die anyway. It is to save yourselves and the rest of the world. You have to understand that. Otherwise you had better go while there is time."

That stopped Prescott and I didn't blame him. He had been five tortured days staggering through the worst bush in Africa to rescue a lunatic.

"You talk to him, Weathers," he said.

"Okay," I replied. "I'll try." So I put it to the priest that here were thirty men who had been sent to rescue him. They were soldiers and they had to obey orders. The position in which they found themselves was militarily untenable. To stay there meant their deaths. He could save their lives by agreeing to leave the mission before Schwartz and his men got there. Therefore he ought to put his own stubborn pride aside and agree to leave the mission to save the lives of others. It was a pretty good effort, but it didn't have the slightest effect on Father Felix. Everybody could leave. He would be quite content to see them go. He had to stay.

I made a final effort, attacking him on his pet subject. "Look," I said, "I know that you have a hang-up on abortion and world population problems. Do you think these men should be commanded to make a stand here to defend your narrow positions on these topics? Men shouldn't

[*99*]

have to lay down their lives to defend the convictions of bigots."

"Abortion," he said almost in wonderment. "I should have thought of that." For a moment I thought he was going to be reasonable and so did Prescott, but he wasn't.

"You mean your decision to stay here isn't to publicize your views on that subject?" I asked.

"Of course not," he replied. "This isn't the place that battle is going to be fought—not at all. And I don't want anyone to stay here who doesn't want to stay." He paused and looked around.

"This is a place of peace," he went on. "Over there the dead are buried. Over there the children are educated, and over there they are fed. There is a hospital for the sick. And out there, we grow our food. That's why I'm staying here. To give the world—the whole world—a chance to defend such a place as this. The world has never had that chance clearly before. It is always 'defend Berlin' or 'defend Paris' or 'defend London.' Always some military or political consideration. But there is no military consideration involved here. Nothing political, either. Nothing strategic or commercial or popular. No valuable mine or centers of commerce. Nothing of the sort. This place belongs to all mankind—surely you can appreciate that. It's quite easy to understand, if you will just think about it. Don't think of a Catholic mission. Think of what we do here. We feed people, we clothe them, we educate them, we tend them when they are sick, we give them love and when they die we bury them and we pray for them. It isn't a military target at all, you see, that I'm giving the world a chance to defend. It is humanity itself. That's it. Humanity itself. Surely it is time that we started to defend humanity itself. It's getting late, you know. There isn't much time left."

That stopped us. Bomba was still standing there with the dirty enameled basin in his hand, in which there were a few kernels left. Prescott looked about at the miserable mud walls, absolutely dazed by what the priest had said and the kind of fortress in which he had been called upon to defend "humanity itself." I was stupefied. I'd gone for the abortion story hook, line and sinker, the complete sophisticate able to spot a bigot in every Roman collar. And here was this ridiculous figure of a priest in a solar topee making a lunatic statement which contained values that I had forgotten about ages ago.

Prescott broke the spell. He stared at the priest, turned abruptly and strode to the compound wall, glared over it and strode back again. He looked at the mission building with a professional eye and said suddenly, "What are you all standing around there for? Get that Vickers up on the roof."

I glanced at Father Felix and said, "Son of a bitch." It was my turn, after all.

Prescott now won my complete admiration. I had no use for him in his disguise as officer and gentleman, or in his other role, the grenade-draped white mercenary whooping it up in the local nightclubs. But as a soldier he was tremendous, and please do not forget that this was not my first war. He got the Vickers up on the roof in less than an hour, surrounded by sandbags and with a commanding sweep of the northwestern approach to the mission. He reinforced the roof under the machine gun and put three tiers of sandbags over the top of it so that it was secure against anything but a direct hit through the firing slit, from mortar fire.

He put half his men to filling sandbags and the other half to digging foxholes and putting the sandbags along the compound wall. There was a ton and a half of hay and other fodder in a lean-to against the back of the mission and he had that moved and scattered about the compound so that it couldn't be set on fire in a stack and burn the mission down. He went through every building getting rid of anything that could be set alight, and every container that could be used for the purpose was filled with water and put about the place, for drinking and dousing fires. He inspected the hospital, grunted with satisfaction over the earth floor and had two bare wooden cupboards put outside the building. When Father Felix remonstrated about this Prescott said curtly, "Anything wood splinters, and splinters are as bad as shrapnel."

In short, he went through the whole mission and converted it by the end of the day into a fort that might have commanded the approval of Wellington, who was an expert on forts.

Father Felix didn't like this at all. In fact he told Prescott to stop because he was destroying the mission with his defense preparations. Prescott replied, "Padre, if I have to defend this place, I'm going to do a professional job of it."

The only concession he made to the priest was to leave the flag up there on its pole—the banner of the Sacred Heart. He was about to order it taken down when he caught the priest's eye, so he left it. But he made use of it too. He moved it with its pole so that it stood right by the machine-gun nest on the top of the roof, and when I blurted out that that was a piece of complete asininity because it made a magnificent ranging mark for the mortar, he said, "Precisely. Schwartz will never believe that I put a ranging mark right beside my only machine-gun nest. He'll zero in on everything but that flag. Alsatian, you know. They have no imagination at all."

As the day wore on, and the defenses of the mission

mounted, Schwartz became more and more of a figure of menace. It was nothing anybody said. It was, I think, the care taken over our defenses and also the fact that I was very tired and away from all the comfort of familiar surroundings. It is surprising how much inner strength one gets out of the presence of familiar places and people. At the bar of the Shamrock Club the mention of the name Schwartz would scarcely have produced any reaction on my part, and even if I had been given elaborate details of his delight in atrocity, I would have shrugged it all off as propaganda. But now I began to recall those pictures of heaps of human limbs with dogs sniffing around them, and the human heads strung from poles, with the string passing through the eye sockets. That was the legitimate Schwartz touch—the degradation of humanity; mockery of the plight of the dead.

At one time in that long afternoon the thought occurred to me that all I had to do was walk out. I didn't have to be penned up in this place awaiting disaster. Of course there was that frightful forest beyond and then the swamp with the saw grass. But people can survive these things. There wasn't really anything to prevent me from strolling off over the sandbags and across the bridge into the forest.

But I didn't. No noble sentiment prevented me from going. It was the hens. Huge, giant black Bomba had taken a fancy to the hens. They were, I think, Rhode Island Reds. The hens in turn seemed to have taken a fancy to him, perhaps because he was the last person to feed them. But wherever he went, there were the hens, clucking and pecking about his huge feet. That barnyard touch in the midst of our preparation for slaughter kept me from leaving. Bomba suited the hens and the hens suited him. I stayed.

When the mission had been fortified, and trip wires

had been set out on the expected approaches of Schwartz —trip wires linked to hand grenades—Prescott busied himself with the radiotelephone. It was vital that we get the thing working.

Prescott, of course, needed to get in touch with Maikap, report his position and say that he was trying to defend a mission which was about as strong as a wet cardboard box. I wanted to get through to New York and report that we were defending humanity on behalf of the whole world.

But the radiotelephone wouldn't work. Finally, under strictest questioning and promises that no punishment would be inflicted, one of the men admitted that he had dropped it. Not all of it. Just a part. That had broken some circuit in its delicate insides.

Prescott removed a couple of panels and tried to trace the wiring, but it was too much for him. Back in the compound we dragged out the kerosene can again, muffled it in the blanket and our drummer started to make it "talk." We all listened. After repeated callings, followed by periods of intense listening, we heard a faint drumbeat in return. Some kind of conversation took place, with our drummer repeating whatever he was "saying" several times. At the end of it he reported the news to us.

"Three villages have been burned on this side of the river. Everybody left but some old men who were hung. Schwartz is one day away."

Immediately after we received this news, one of the hens hopped up on the radiotelephone and relieved itself over its delicate interior wiring.

Chapter
Twelve

NOTHING happened for a whole day. We stood about in
the fortified mission, sweltering in the muggy heat, blinded
by the light, sweating, watching and mumbling to each
other, everybody getting on everybody's nerves. Meals
were taken in shifts so that the Vickers and the Bren and
BAR posts were manned, and Prescott went to work on
that radiotelephone with its lumpish batteries which could
now be recharged by the mission generator. That proved
a blind alley, and, giving up, he improvised a grenade
launcher which was wildly inaccurate but could fling a
grenade about two hundred yards. It was constructed on
the principle of the automatic pitching machine used by
ball clubs, itself designed on the principle of the ballista,
a Roman machine for throwing stones. It impressed the
men but it was of dubious worth, for when a live grenade

was hurled from it, the missile exploded fifty feet up in the air, panicking Father Felix's two cows.

Father Felix was the only one who was not on edge. He was a little testy but that was because of the fortification of the mission, which he had not anticipated. He was angry about the cows left grazing in the pasture, and went out to bring them back in. But Prescott forbade this. "They are my pickets, Padre," he said. "They'll give us first warning when Schwartz is near."

"They are quite used to people coming here down the forest road," said the priest. "They won't show any sign at all."

"The tick birds will," said Prescott. "When there is someone coming, they'll hop down off their backs. And that man there"—pointing to a soldier on the roof with a pair of field glasses—"is watching the tick birds."

A good soldier, Captain Prescott, as you see.

Prescott made no more attempts to get Father Felix to leave the mission. In his seamy life he had fought for many a dubious cause. He had decided now to fight for the priest. I think this was, to a large degree, a case of professionalism. A professional, after all, takes pride in his work. He likes to feel that he is exercising his skill for some worthwhile end. In Prescott's case that worthwhile end had for a long time been money. Now, however, he had a chance to use his experience and talent on behalf of something less shabby. Humanity. It was a glowing word. It raised the soldier to the level of the knight—or what the knight was intended to be.

Don't forget Prescott's preoccupation with his image as officer and gentleman—English officer and gentleman. I think that defending the mission gave him a chance to

[106]

play in uniform the part he had so often played in "mufti," as he liked to put it.

He'd changed a bit, or maybe I was getting used to him and he getting used to me. At sunset he offered me another drink of whisky. I had to sit at a table in the mission office, which he had turned into his headquarters, while glasses were brought, and water as well. He had his ritual. There was no question of taking a slug out of the flask. A soldier stood by in the corner like a waiter. That was part of the ritual. These things were important to Prescott. After he'd examined the pale gold of the whisky in the glow of the lamplight and said, "Cheers," and taken a gulp, he went on, "Queer place to wind up, isn't it? You from wherever you come from and me from—England. With a mad priest and a bunch of wogs in the worst part of Africa."

"Where in England do you come from?" I asked.

He hesitated, ruminating, I think, over some lie he had probably been telling all his life. Then he put the lie aside. "Wigan," he said. "It's in Lancashire. It's a dirty, wet, smoky, industrial town near Stockton. I can never remember a sunny day in Wigan."

The whisky relaxed him and he began to talk about himself for the first time—as if he were making a confession. He'd joined the Army, long before World War II, to get out of Wigan, he said; to get out of the raw cold and the clanging trolley cars and the "penn'orth" of fish and chips, carefully hoarded and eaten to the last crumb, and the loneliness of standing on street corners on Saturday nights, watching other people going by in cars. His regiment had been sent to India, and all he told me about India was that he had once been given the job of sawing off the top of the skull of an officer who had died of a fit, so that an examination of the brain could be made for military records.

"How horrifying," I said.

"He was a real bastard," said Prescott. "I enjoyed it."

He shut up then and it really wasn't necessary to tell me much more. In the British Army—in anybody's army, I suppose—the pay is small and promotion works, or used to work, on a caste system. So when World War II was over, he became a mercenary, soldiering being all he knew, and the change from corporal to captain on excellent pay was made in one leap, for evolving Africa had great need of mercenaries. Then came the blue blazer with the regimental crest on the breast pocket, the gray flannels, the clipped military moustache compensated for by predictable nights of stumbling around nightclubs with grenades pinned to his shirt and his gentleman's moustache soaked in native beer.

When he asked where I came from I was tempted, out of compassion, to lie and tell a tale of the Chicago stockyards or the Philadelphia slums. But I told the truth about Princeton and Columbia and a job on *The Wall Street Journal* followed by a stint with a publisher and a gradual drift into writing magazine pieces, with money behind me in case of dry periods.

"Lovely," he said. "Really lovely. I saw you looking over the wall yesterday, thinking of going over the hill, perhaps? Well, I wouldn't blame you—not with that to go back to."

"I have to stay here with Bomba and the hens," I said.

"Blasted hens," he said, recalling perhaps what had happened with the radiotelephone. "I'd like to wring their necks."

[*108*]

I asked him about Schwartz. "He's cracked," he said. "Real bastard. Told me once he used to blind frogs when he was a kid and watch them bash into things when he made them jump. Damned good soldier, mind you."

Father Felix was alone at the mission. We had expected to find at least a few helpers around but he had sent them all away and advised his flock, who lived in little villages scattered mostly on the west bank of the river, to move off into the forest. I don't know what he had planned to do if we did not come. I fancy he would have gone on milking his cows and feeding his chickens and saying his Office until Schwartz arrived and killed him.

Regarding his stand he said little more by way of explanation than he had said on our first arrival. He was giving the world a chance to save itself—to make a stand for humanity. But on the matter of humanity he went a little deeper. "We are becoming mere statistics," he said. "Counted, sorted into groups, classified according to beliefs and earnings and religions and viewpoints and education. We are being prepared for a future role as ants. Yes, ants. Worker ants and soldier ants and builder ants and farmer ants and consumer ants, each given its reward for performance up to the norm and its punishment for failing to reach the norm.

"We are halfway there already. A few steps further and there will be no return. We are undergoing a change in our thinking. That is where the danger lies—a change from human thought to insect thought, from concern for the individual to concern only for the colony. Yes, my friend. Unless we make our stand now, the insects will swallow us."

That evening, leaving the various gun posts manned, Prescott paraded his little force and said a few words to

[*109*]

them in Swahili. Then he stood aside and Father Felix, after a little interval, emerged from his chapel in his white robe and said something further, which I could not understand. When he had finished the men were dismissed; and three or four of them, after conferring, picked up their haversacks and rifles, shook hands with the others and moved out of the compound toward the bridge over the river which would take them into the forest and to the safe side.

"The padre insisted that they be told why they were here and given permission to go if they didn't support his cause," said Prescott. "It's important to him that everybody who stays should be willing to do so and know exactly what he is staying for. Of course it's difficult to talk about the Conscience of the World in Swahili, but they got the general idea."

"Just how did he put it?" I asked.

"He said men must have homes and families and peace and it was time that men fought for these things. They know him anyway, and so they are staying."

"They believed him, then?"

Prescott looked around at his men. "Yes. In the whole world you could say there are two dozen blacks who believe in him."

"And you?"

Prescott shrugged. "I never cared before," he said. "Maybe I'm daft too. But I think he's right."

Chapter
Thirteen

THE sun set behind the tall trees of the forest to the west at about five, and deep shadows of enormous length flowed over the clearing in which the mission stood and dissolved the buildings. A night breeze, very refreshing, sprang up and for a while blew so briskly that we could hear the leaves and branches of the forest rustling like a fleeing multitude. A branch broke with a snap that made everybody jump, and the wind rose higher and then gradually died away. The stars emerged in a sky which but a few moments before had been a thin gold, tinged here and there with mauve.

The mission buildings reappeared, resurrected by starlight. Every upper surface was silver, while the shadows were ebony. Even the foxholes looked beautiful with their pale crescents of earth about them. But Prescott had no eye for this loveliness and, glancing at his beloved Vickers, was pleased to note that the outline of the deadly nest in which it had its home was broken by the shadow of the flag—the banner of the Sacred Heart sorrowing in what was left of the evening breeze.

I was entranced. We are most of us city dwellers and not out often enough in the starlight, which gives a clean and lovely edge to pebbles, to blades of grass, to twigs, to cracks and all the minutiae of the world which are lost in the sun. The sentries squatted at their posts behind the sandbags which lined the low wall of the compound.

They stared across the light-frosted fields to the black void of the forest, which stood thicker than any cloud against the twinkling sky. A little after sunset a wisp of mist appeared over the fields, lying on the surface between the wall and the first of the forest trees. It grew thicker as the air chilled, and soon the whole clearing was clothed in a level swathe of silver mist out of which there jutted here and there, ogrelike, the top of a bush or a straggle of fence posts.

I thought of Tennyson's line: "Clothed in white samite, mystic, wonderful," for the scene was enchanting.

The mist, however, made the soldiers nervous. Not only did it offer cover for their attackers but they held it bad for their health—a belief they had got from the early Portuguese with their talk of malaria—the bad air of the night. The sentries pulled the backs of their bush shirts over their heads, believing it especially important to guard the head against this menace.

I sought Bomba. Prescott was up on the roof with the Vickers, his great love. Bomba, as I have said, was from the Sudan and so he wasn't afraid of the mist, for the people of the Sudan have not been exposed to as many

European superstitions as those of the rest of Africa. He was standing in a dark shadow behind a Bren gun position in the angle of the kitchen wall and he said, "They're out there in the fields now, coming closer."

"How do you know?" I asked.

For answer he took a rifle and, aiming it at one of the monster-like bushes that jutted up above the mist, bade me sight along the barrel. "See it moving?" he asked. "No wind. They're crawling through the mist, guiding themselves by the bushes and fence posts."

"Have you told Captain Prescott?" I asked.

"He knows," he said. "That's why he's up there with the Vickers." I looked about. The little blobs of men at their gun positions behind the sandbags might have been painted there. Nobody stirred. Nobody made a sound.

Then, like some monster surfacing from the depths, Father Felix's gray-brown cow erupted from the mist. It rose, as cows do, backside first—a grotesque triangle of flesh bursting into view—and then up came the back and head and horns, and off it plunged, thundering and mooing through the silvery sea, giving the alarm, as Prescott had said it would.

Immediately a score of heads popped up out of the mist and the whole night was shaken by a volley of fire. Bullets tore like hornets into the compound wall and into the mission walls, into the roof and into the ground about. Standing close to the roof, near Bomba, I was deluged by a shower of shattered tiles and dirt pouring over me. The air was choked with dust, as the bullets ripped into the dried adobe walls; and in a second or two it was impossible to see clearly across the compound to the men lining the sandbagged wall.

Nobody on our side replied—a tremendous tribute to

Prescott's discipline. That gigantic volley rose to a peak, held it and then died away to a few ragged little discharges. Then silence. And then cheers of exultation from the attackers and shouts and laughter, for they believed the mission deserted.

Schwartz, however, was not the man to run readily into a trap; and one after another, so rapidly that there was surely hardly a second between explosions, half a dozen mortar shells were dropped into the compound. They would have done horrid damage but for the foxholes. One went through the mission roof, blew a hole in the walls and sent a door cartwheeling across the compound like an exuberant clown. When there was no reply to this, there was another outburst of cheering; and the attackers, throwing all caution aside, rushed for the compound wall, firing their weapons out of sheer jubilation.

It was only then that the Vickers spoke, and I saw immediately why Prescott loved it. It mowed men down like a scythe—not just the front line of men, but those five, ten and fifteen paces behind. Some leaped into the air like trout. Some crashed backwards to disappear in the mist as if they had been hit by a battering ram. Others jerked, jumped, flipped and crumpled before that terrible leaden scythe which chattered away on the mission roof. The automatic rifles that joined in were a mere boys' chorus to the stentorian solo of the Vickers. The attackers, screaming, yelling, rushed the wall. More mortar shells came whistling against the stars to drop into the compound. Between dust, mist and smoke the air became thicker and thicker and the whole attack a vast blurred pandemonium, lit by the explosion of mortar shells, the lightning crisscross of tracers and at last by the moon, which rose huge and golden in the eastern sky.

A whole wave of men reached the wall. I saw half a dozen at least get to the top in one place and then tumble off, some outside and some inside. A mortar shell hit one part of the wall squarely and it disappeared into dust. I crouched in the angle of the kitchen wall and caught grotesque glimpses of the battle: Bomba laughing as at some huge joke and spitting the firing pin of a grenade from between his teeth; one of Father Felix's Rhode Island Reds flapping up to the roof, its behind looking like a feather duster in the moonlight; a black foot with its white sole stuck out of a foxhole where a head should be; and the dirty enamel basin from which Father Felix fed his hens, leaping about the compound as it was hit by one bullet and then another. It finally took a great leap into the air and disappeared over the wall, as if fleeing to safety.

It was quite impossible to say who was winning and who was losing. Then, from out in the fields, there came three sharp blasts on a whistle and the attack petered out. The Vickers stopped its authoritative chatter, the lighter rattle of the automatic rifles died away. One more mortar shell whistled against the stars and plummeted into the compound and the firing ended. The air cleared and the disturbed mist settled back over the fields. But there was no longer silence out there. Instead there were cries and groans, and one appalling scream of pure terror. I saw a man rise above the mist, his hands clasped to his stomach, presumably to keep his entrails in. He stumbled forward, head and shoulders, for a few paces and then went down into the folds of that beautiful shroud.

All during the attack I had not seen Father Felix. I think he was in his chapel. But he appeared now in that white robe and started immediately to attend to the wounded. We had three men badly hit, six slightly hurt and two dead. Father Felix had a chest of surgical instruments which were probably as old as he was, and there were plenty of bandages made from the mission sheets.

As the only other civilian present I plainly had to help him. He was crude but competent. He poured a quantity of a disinfectant called Jeyes fluid into a basin, tumbled the instruments into it and started to work. He took the worst cases first and did not apply that old battlefield rule of tending first to those he knew he could save. He could tell at a glance which man was in the worst condition and that was the man who got attention, my job being to stop whatever bleeding I could among the others.

He had no anesthetic and so he had some of the uninjured men hold the patient while he probed and swabbed. The screams would have unnerved many a lesser man, but he worked on unmoved, saying a word now and then to the patient or to those holding him. But he never seemed to have to hesitate. His big, old man's hands, with their loose bones, worked confidently and firmly on the young black flesh. When he had finished he asked whether there were others, and being told there were none he went to the door to get his first breath of fresh air since the end of the battle. The mist still clung to the ground and standing at the door he heard the groans of Schwartz's men out beyond the way.

"You told me there were no more," he said indignantly and without another word strode across the compound and staggered up the sandbags and over the wall into the mist. Prescott was furious and ordered him back, but Father Felix took no notice. On he went, waist-deep in the fog, headed for sounds of moaning nearby. There was nothing to do but follow him.

"Christ," said Prescott. "Come back. You don't know Schwartz. He's using those men for bait." I was a yard or two behind the priest and, sure enough, a second later there was that appalling whistle against the stars, and a mortar shell crumpled into the ground so close to the priest that he was knocked down by the blast and, I thought, killed. But he was up in a moment on his hands and knees and crawling toward the wounded man.

The faithful practice of cowardice had preserved my life in many dangers up to then, but cowardice proved me false at this point. I should have run. Every hair on my body was standing stiffly erect and my skin felt as if it had wrinkled up like a walnut. Indeed I should have run, but I didn't. Fear of showing my fear chained me to the priest. So, sanity deserting me, I crawled to the wounded man, and between the two of us, we got him halfway erect and started to carry him back to the compound.

At any moment I expected to be split open like a herring by mortar fire, or perhaps sawed in half by an automatic rifle. I cursed the wounded man and I cursed Father Felix. I prayed and made extravagant promises to whatever deity there might possibly be with an interest in me, to spare my life. And between cursing and praying and the imminent expectation of death, we got the man to the compound and over the wall. He died the moment we got him inside.

Father Felix saw that he was dead and went out to get another. I stood there calling to him to come back, but on he waded through the mist, with no more concern for himself than if he were going to milk a cow. Bomba had come up to help us get the man over the wall and stood looking at me. So I went over the wall after the priest, and if you wonder at my behavior then I will remind you

[*117*]

that it was Solomon who remarked that it is pride that kills men. Bomba started to follow but Prescott yelled to him to stay where he was.

"That's just what Schwartz wants," he said. "Half a dozen of you out there. I'll shoot the next man that goes over that wall."

This time it was a little bit better. Nobody fired at us and the man we got in didn't die, though he ought to have died, for he was missing a hand and half his foot and his legs were broken. We got seven in all and weren't fired at. Three died but that couldn't be helped, and when they were all brought in Father Felix started work on them.

He was consoled that we hadn't been fired at and thought this a sign of compassion on the part of our enemies.

Prescott shook his head. "You don't know Schwartz," he said.

Chapter
Fourteen

WE tried to get the radiotelephone to work again—or rather Prescott tried and Father Felix tried. The batteries were fully charged, and everything was hooked up, but it was dead.

I had no hope for the thing. I had the curious feeling that at some time, undefined, we had passed out of the consciousness of the world and all possibility of contact with it. I think this happened when we passed over that swaying bridge of vines and bamboo leading from the forest across the river to the little clearing in which the mission stood. The radiotelephone would work if we were back on the road again with the half-tracks; in short, if it could recognize around it some signs of the world of science to which it belonged. But in this primeval world of mist, mud, blood and fright it wouldn't work because it was in the wrong place to work.

Ridiculous thoughts, of course. But I was terribly tired, as was everybody else, and sleep brought no refreshment. Sleep was a mere resting of the muscles and the blood—a mere physical resting. The brain, the mind, did not rest at all. My sleep was more horrid than my waking, for in my waking there was always Bomba, still with his pink-and-white smile in his big black face, still able, it seemed, to recharge himself with energy from the sun.

Awake there was also Father Felix. I now began to understand the position of the Jews during their forty Biblical years in the wilderness. Their real comfort was not God but Moses. Every time Moses went away, the Jews fell to pieces and forgot what they were there for and became completely demoralized. And although no great believer in the divinity myself, if it weren't for Father Felix, I would have become completely demoralized too. I would have sneaked away or pleaded for surrender or done anything at all to put an end to the nightmare. I hadn't run off before because of the hens. That now seemed to me madness. There were only three hens left. The rest had been killed in one way or another during that first furious assault.

They weren't contented, clucking, happy hens anymore. They were panicked and stupefied, and one of them just crouched to the ground, wings slightly outspread and trembling as if guarding her chickens. Bomba did something worth recording. He got some fairly roundish stones and slipped them under her to give her the feeling of eggs, and some of the trembling stopped. Bomba understood both the hens and Father Felix's position far, far better than I. I understood it as an ethic. He understood it as a reality. I could talk about Love. He could feel the heartbeat.

There was a special kinship of sorts between Father Felix and Bomba, between the tall, unbending, strong, old white priest and the massive, strong, healthy, fighting black. Bomba was a fine fighter. He fought with joy, unafraid, as if mortal combat were a natural activity of a creature called Man.

The Vickers was Prescott's favorite weapon. If you feel any fondness for Bomba I still have to tell you that his favorite weapon was the grenade. He hurled it with power and accuracy and effect, and altered the timing on a number of grenades so that they could be hurled from the makeshift launcher without exploding harmlessly in midflight. He positioned the launcher on the back slope of a little knoll close to the cemetery area and put some sandbags behind it. He launched a grenade or two from it and was able to delay the timing so that they didn't burst until they hit the edge of the forest. This brought a shift in the mortar fire, giving that whistling menace another place to probe. It had found the Vickers and thoroughly pounded it. The roof of the mission around was gone and the whole machine-gun nest would have tumbled through to the ground below but for the excellent underpinning of timber and sandbags which Prescott had contrived.

One of the men on the Vickers crew was, however, hit by a mortar fragment which broke his jaw and made a bloody, spongy mess of the bone and flesh of his mouth. But the Vickers remained unhurt and waiting for its next chance to strike. The mortar pounded away at utterly irrational intervals. There would be periods of an hour or more when it was silent, and then there would be five or six shells in quick succession, all on one area, and then silence again.

The unwounded men stayed in the foxholes or, if in the

open, flattened out immediately upon hearing the whistle of the mortar shell. The wounded were compelled to stay in their beds enduring their agony and expecting to be blown to pieces the next time a covey of shells came over. Father Felix spent most of the day with them. He took no notice of the intermittent bombardment at all, and he kept everything as normal as possible.

The hospital floor was soon littered with dust and debris from the bombardment, and despite the fact that more dust and debris were to be expected for a great length of time, Father Felix got a broom and swept it clean. He said Mass as usual and asked Prescott to inform the men of the time in case any wished to attend. Several did. Three of the wounded men, it turned out, were Catholics, Catholicism being the traditional religion of the Portuguese, and he heard their confessions, absolved their sins and brought them Communion.

He continued to care for the surviving hens. At his "cluck cluck cluck" the remnant of them gathered about him (even the one that had lain so panicked with outstretched wings) and he fed them—though behind the mission building, where there was a little protection from the insane firing of the mortar. He buried the dead in individual graves, and made a record in a vast journal in his office of which grave contained which body: "Llango, aged about nineteen, of the village of Koti, province of Kumonga, killed in defense of humanity. He is buried with Catholic rites in the first grave to the left on entering the cemetery from the north gate. Bugali, aged about twenty-three. . . ." So the entries went.

"The world's first real scroll of honor," he said, showing me the entries. "These are the first men to fall knowingly and willingly in the only cause worth fighting for."

The graves of the dead of Schwartz's men were also carefully noted, but lacked the phrase "Killed in defense of humanity."

Prescott, by midafternoon, had decided that the mortar must be destroyed. He had pinpointed its position but efforts to hit it with the grenade launcher were so wildly inaccurate as to be hilarious. The thing, in baseball terms, threw sliders, knuckle balls, curve balls, screwballs, anything but a fast ball straight down the middle, which was what was required. The trouble lay not in the launcher itself but in the shape of the grenade, which was not designed for long-distance, high-velocity hurling.

The obvious man to send to destroy the mortar was Bomba, the grenade expert; and when the forest shadows had flowed over the clearing and touched the mission wall, he gave me his pink-and-white grin, gave a cluck or two to the hens and slipped over the compound wall, draped in grenades so spaced that they would not click against one another in moving.

I followed his shape around the angle of the wall. He moved with an easy velvety motion like a black leopard, if there is such a creature, and then he was gone. I tried to follow him with field glasses—an excellent pair of Zeiss night glasses, which were the personal property of Prescott—but could not find him. He had taken with him a considerable length of clothesline, for some purpose which I could not divine, and also one of those small British bayonets which are really more dagger than sword and which first made their appearance at the beginning of World War II. Its use was quite obvious. In Bomba's fat fist it would be a terrible weapon.

I trained the glasses on a clump of thorns behind which the mortar lay, and after a while I fancied I could see them move, imperceptibly at first and then with sudden vigor. Immediately there was an explosion of automatic rifle fire and I could see the thornbushes being ripped and torn to twigs. Then there came, almost within the space of a second, it seemed, four sharp explosions with light violet centers, and then one more. Again there was a volley from the automatics, and then three more explosions and then, for a while, nothing.

A few minutes later, however, the whole edge of the forest erupted into firing, the flash of the rifles looking like a firefly display against the dark of the forest. This died down and we waited and waited until after half an hour there came a slight hiss and Bomba said, "It's me." In a moment he had dropped over the wall, a little out of breath and very pleased.

"I got it," he said to Prescott. "Three grenades—right inside the sandbags. It's finished."

I asked him whether it had not been a near thing for him, blundering into the thornbushes, and he grinned happily. "They should never have fallen for that," he said. "That's the oldest trick there is. I tied that clothesline to the thorns, moved off and pulled on it, and when they opened fire I knew just where to throw the first grenades."

"Very good work," said Prescott. "How many?"

"About six," said Bomba. "But there's maybe a hundred."

We were all very pleased and began to feel that it was just possible that we were not doomed. I began to hope that perhaps a relief column would be sent down to us from Maikap. After all, Utori must be getting anxious, I reasoned, not having heard anything from us for several days. Thinking a little more deeply, however, with my knowledge of Utori, I realized I was quite wrong in thinking he would be anxious about us. His view would be an entirely practical one. He had sent a detachment of men to defend the mission "in the name of humanity." He had answered the call to the "Conscience of the World." If the detachment were wiped out that would be better propaganda for his cause than if it succeeded. If it succeeded, the incident would soon be forgotten in the hurlyburly of the world's affairs. If the effort failed, it would be remembered. Remember Thermopylae. Remember the Alamo. The heroic last stands live on.

Had we, I wondered, been expendable from the start? Any fool can benefit from a victory. But it takes a truly great man to arrange a profitable defeat. And Utori was certainly a great man.

Chapter
Fifteen

SINCE his first conversation with Father Felix, feeding his hens so peacefully in the compound yard, Prescott had said nothing further about evacuation or surrender. He was quite content that the long road from Wigan, the thirty years of soldiering and of slaughter, should end in this defense of the mission. Perhaps everybody in the world has a sacred grail, some conscious of it, and some not. Perhaps some recognize it, "seeing the light" in the time-worn phrase, but decide that the prize is too difficult to grasp or the time too late. I think Prescott had "seen the light" now. The defense of Father Felix and the mission made sense of his life, which up to that time had been nothing more than a flight from the wet, raw, smoky streets of Wigan.

He was as military as ever—to a degree, more so. He

took to saluting the priest every time he met him or they passed each other. He never called him by name but always referred to him by the title "The Padre." And that title, coupled with the sight of the old priest in the white robe of the Dominicans, still wearing, when out in the sun, that solar topee which belonged to the last century, transformed him for all of us into a noble and august presence. Even when he was in seclusion, his personality, or something of him, was still among us. Between Bomba and the priest the relationship was different. Certainly Bomba did not lack respect for Father Felix, but he was on easier terms with him. They understood each other as water understands water. With Prescott there was the sense of service and deep respect.

For myself, I was the least influenced by the personality of Father Felix. I now believed him to be sincere in his stand, and a little mad too. But I also believed that he was merely a propaganda piece for Utori, and however noble his own ideals, they would eventually be used merely to serve the purpose of rallying world support to Utori's Republican government.

I took Prescott aside and discussed this with him. He brushed the whole thing off with professional scorn. "You can't expect me to think like a civilian," he said. "If a soldier starts examining the political motives behind his orders, he isn't a soldier anymore. The only thing to do is carry out orders. That's all. My orders are to defend the mission and the Padre."

"To the last man?" I asked.

"Certainly," he said.

"Listen, Prescott," I said, "if Father Felix told you to surrender, would you surrender?"

"Of course," he said. "The Padre is in command. When

he didn't want anyone staying who didn't want to stay, I obeyed his orders, and let them go. At that time the men knew they would have to make a stand to the last. You could have gone then too, you know. You can still go now, I suppose."

"I have a profession as well as you," I replied. "However, I do not hold myself obliged to stay to the last man."

"Or the last hen," said Prescott. He was developing quite a sense of humor.

I decided to discuss the matter with Father Felix. I felt I had to show him how it was quite possible he was being used, and was allowing men to be killed in a hopeless situation for purely political purposes. He was so busy that his only leisure moments were when he was asleep, but I cornered him in the kitchen and told him I had to talk to him privately. We went to the shambles of his study, and I told him my suspicion that it was possibly Utori's cold-blooded intention that everybody at the mission should die for propaganda purposes.

"I have known Utori for a long time and I think that is possible," he said calmly. "But that is really a side issue. The world knows that we are besieged here now. Some will say we are making a stand for one thing, some for another. But the truth will eventually come out—that it is humanity itself we are defending—men's concern for their fellowmen—man's compassion for man. Whether Utori decides to use it for propaganda doesn't really matter. The men who have stayed know the truth and they will die if need be for that truth."

This conversation took place early in the morning after Bomba had wiped out the mortar. We had had an anxious night of it, but a peaceful one. The mist had gathered, the forest beyond had receded into darkness, the bushes and fence posts had loomed grotesque through the silver flooring of fog. There had been one or two irritated bursts of automatic fire from the enemy, but no serious assault.

One of the first tasks of the morning, when men could be spared, was to dig graves for two of the wounded who had died during the night. Father Felix and I were interrupted at the end of our conversation by the news that the graves were ready and Captain Prescott was assembling the off-duty men for the funeral service.

Father Felix left to officiate at the burials but I remained behind, though I knew that this would bring a reprimand from Prescott, who took it as "poor form" for anyone to absent himself from a funeral.

My mind was quite muddled. It was all very well for Prescott to find his fulfillment in the defense of the mission. It was all very well for Father Felix to remain to the death if need be to awaken the conscience of the world, but I had no function there unless I survived to tell the tale. If my function was to survive, then it was professionally important for me to get away, whether Prescott understood this or not. What is the use of an Alamo unless there is a survivor to record the glorious deed?

I had just arrived at this satisfying and obvious conclusion when I heard a sound which I had come to fear—the high-pitched whistle of a mortar shell. It was followed by several others, and a series of explosions shook the mission, and once again the air was filled with shouts and screams, with smoke and dust and confusion.

I was so terrified that I just sat where I was, like a startled rabbit, in the priest's study, while the roof rained dust and tiles on me, while the walls shook and the ground trembled, and figures rushed past the shattered windows, glimpsed for a second and then gone.

The bombardment went on for several minutes, and I cursed Bomba, for he hadn't exterminated Schwartz's terrible mortar after all. When the shelling stopped, I rushed out for the comfort of company and, glancing up, saw the black snout of the machine gun move like an awakened snake in its hole and men manning the various posts around the compound wall. There came another new bombardment, but this time of smoke shells, which, landing in the mission compound and immediately before it, deprived us of our vision. I thought for a while that they were gas shells, for the smoke was so thick as to set me and others coughing violently. But apart from that they did us no harm. We sucked the fouled air cautiously through nose and mouth and strained to see the attackers we knew must be racing toward us behind that screen.

Prescott was still master of the situation. "They will take three minutes," he shouted. "I want a five-second burst from everybody in three minutes' time. I will give the order." I peered around but couldn't see him. "Steady, everybody," he said. "We'll get them this time. Just keep your heads."

That was an appallingly long three minutes. Several times in eddies of the smoke which in the windless air billowed before us, I thought I saw figures approaching. At any moment I expected the billows of smoke to explode in volley after volley of bullets. I was crouched behind the sandbags around the compound wall and debated whether I wouldn't be safer in the mission. I was about to make a run for it when again there came that whistling of mortar shells which I dreaded so much, and the compound was stitched with half a dozen of them. I heard a terrible clattering and assumed that a large portion of the mission wall had fallen. Then, when the last of the mortar shells had fallen, Prescott blew his whistle and immediately the Vickers started its heavy slow chatter and the automatic rifles hosed their bullets into the smoke.

Prescott had his timing exactly right. When that last mortar shell fell, Schwartz's men got up for the charge and, meeting our well-timed fire, they went down in windrows. We heard their screams and cries, though we couldn't see them, and the five seconds of fire that Prescott had called for went on far beyond that time.

The smoke of the mortar barrage began to clear, and a number of attackers flung themselves over the wall just a few feet to my right where a round from the mortar had made a breach. They spread out rapidly and were followed by others, fanning out and squirting bullets at anything they saw. Bomba lobbed two grenades among them. Several went down and the rest fled.

There were two more penetrations that I could see, of even greater numbers, but they failed for lack of reinforcement. The Vickers narrowed its sweep to the breach and obliterated the invaders. Then the firing died, the cries and the moans remained and the attackers withdrew. We had twice driven them back. But this time we had paid a very high price. We had lost Prescott.

Prescott was still alive when we found him, but he was terribly mangled. He had taken a burst from an automatic rifle and was drenched with blood. We carried him into the hospital and laid him on the only bed that was left. He was dying and there was nothing that could be done for him. A lot of people gathered around, the men holding back a bit so that Father Felix, Bomba and I were closest to him. His eyes were open and his face impassive. To Bomba he said quite calmly, "You'll have to take over. Use your best judgment. No help coming, I'm afraid.

None whatever." Then he looked at Father Felix and said in his best officer and gentleman accent, "Delighted to have met you, Padre. Delighted."

He looked at me last, but he didn't say anything at all. I supposed at the time that he just couldn't think of anything appropriate. Later I remembered how at our first clash I had told him that his reputation would depend on what I told the world he was, and I thought that he might have been afraid, in these last moments of life, of saying something that would damage that verdict of mine.

Well, I arrived at that verdict, and I put it on the grave where we buried him. It read:

Captain Howard Prescott,
Blemi Republican Army
Officer and Gentleman.

Maybe Prescott really wasn't a gentleman. Certainly in that blazer and those flannels of his with the silk scarf tied around his neck and his clipped military moustache, he was nothing but a snob. But a gentleman was what he wanted to be, and are we really to be blamed if, in trying to attain our heart's desire, we take the wrong road? It is not, after all, the achievement of the Grail that matters. It is the longing and the searching for it. Surely we fail only when we lose the vision and stop trying.

Chapter
Sixteen

ALL now rested on the broad shoulders and the massive physique of Bomba, who seemed to draw his energy from the sun and his strength from the earth. I do not want to make him into a symbol of something; he was much too natural for such contrivances. He was not, for instance, a symbol of Nature, but a product of Nature, a strong, healthy, balanced fruit of the earth, free of all neuroses and artificial loyalties, clear of the curious sickness of cities which compels every man to wear a mask.

He picked up the command easily, saw that the breach in the wall was closed with more sandbags, checked the battered protection of the Vickers, inventoried the ammunition and counted noses. We had eight sound men left, and there were not enough beds in the hospital for all the wounded.

We went out again, Father Felix and I, to get those who had fallen outside the mission walls, but only two of them lived, despite the priest's efforts. Of dead, including the attackers, we had eleven in all and I suggested that surely the time had now come for mass graves. But Father Felix would not hear of it. Each man must have his own resting place, each his own marker; the name of each must be distinctly mentioned, if known, in the funeral service.

The two attacks had taken their toll among others as well. We had now but one surviving hen. Bomba made a pet of it, picked it up and stroked it with that huge hand of his which flung the grenades with such accuracy. We ate the other hens and Bomba ate his share with good appetite, as did Father Felix.

When our defenses had once more been put into shape, Bomba, sitting in the shade and drinking with gusto from a large enameled saucepan containing half a gallon of water, beckoned me over to him. "Next time they come," he said, "we won't be able to hold them off. Unless we get help."

"We'll get no help," I replied.

He nodded his huge head in agreement, looked up at the banner of the Sacred Heart still fluttering above the mission, though riddled by mortar fragments, spat copiously into the dust before him and said, "There's three things we can do. We can hold out until there's none of us left and then they'll get the priest anyway. We can launch a sneak attack of our own when the mist comes and surprise them. Schwartz wouldn't be expecting that. Or we could ask for terms."

"I got the distinct idea that Schwartz isn't the one to grant terms," I said, very surprised.

"That's true," said Bomba. "He's a son of a bitch. But

we could ask him anyway. We could see what he has to say. We don't have to believe him."

"Father Felix wouldn't surrender," I said.

Bomba examined his huge fist, clenching and unclenching it. Then he gave me his surprising pink-and-white smile. "I'm the boss now," he said.

It was agreed that I would take a white flag down to Schwartz and see whether he would offer terms of surrender and, if so, what terms. Father Felix made no objection. That certainly surprised me, but I thought that perhaps his seeing so many of the wounded die, and having to bury them and enter their names on his "Scroll of Honor," was affecting his resolve.

"Tell them we have plenty of ammunition. They can send someone to see for themselves," said Bomba as I left. "Tell them the Vickers is working well," he added chuckling. "They know that anyway."

So off I went, carrying over my head a piece of white cloth on a stick, my heart in my mouth, expecting to be fired upon at any moment, but nothing of the sort happened. A loud-hailer called out in Swahili as I approached Schwartz's position and I replied in English. I was told to stay where I was with the flag held up; and three men came out to me, guns ready, searched me in a perfunctory fashion and took me to Schwartz. He was lying on a camp cot in a tent with the flaps up, and I was quite unprepared for his appearance.

I had expected somehow a brutal, heavy, cruel-looking man, but he was one of the handsomest men I had ever seen. I suppose he was at least my age, though he looked twenty years younger, and he spoke English with a slight accent which had a certain charm. I had visualized black hair, perhaps because his name meant "black," but his

[*137*]

hair was fair and fine, brushed back from the forehead and parted on one side, and that contributed to his boyish look.

"Ah, Weathers," he said. "A delight to meet you, I assure you. So distinguished a person in my poor dwelling. And how is the good Padre? Still saying his prayers, I suppose, and looking forward to the conversion of more and more little black babies?"

"He's well," I said and added, "as tough as ever."

"Prester John himself," said Schwartz. "A legend before his time. Have a drink—the whisky is Japanese but not that bad." He barked a word or two in Swahili and glasses and a bottle were brought. While he served me he said, eyeing the whisky with appreciation as it poured into my glass, "I don't suppose the good priest is the one who suggested this parley?"

"No," I said.

He seemed a little disappointed but went on pouring. "Prescott send you?" he asked.

"Prescott's dead," I replied. "He was killed in the last attack."

"Really," said Schwartz, handing me my glass. "Buried in his blazer, I trust. All the touching sentiments preserved to the last." He laughed delightedly. "Did you ever see him when he was drunk? Dear old Prescott. Cheers."

He put his glass down delicately on the table and said almost in a whisper, "And who, my dear Weathers, is in command now—you?"

"No," I said. "Lieutenant Bomba."

"Bomba," he repeated. He looked puzzled, scratched his cheek with a forefinger and tugged at one of his ear lobes. "Bomba. You know, Weathers, much as I adore our black brothers here in Africa, and I might add that our black sisters are not that bad either, I have a terrible time remembering the names of black officers. Bomba. No, I don't know Bomba."

"Yes, you do," I replied. "He blew up your mortar the other night."

"Touché," said Schwartz. "Very good. Bomba did that, eh? Well, I must remember Lieutenant Bomba. And what is the object of this parley?"

"He sent me to see on what terms you would accept surrender of the mission," I replied. "He told me to say that he has plenty of ammunition, plenty of grenades and, in particular, that the Vickers is in first-class condition."

"Well," said Schwartz, "if he has all that there is no reason to talk about terms, so I will assume that he hasn't. I've lost, between dead and wounded, twenty-three men and, the odds being always in favor of defenders, I will assume that he has lost fifteen. That would leave him perhaps ten left and Prescott gone. Dear Prescott. You're sure they buried him in his blazer? If not, I think he ought to be dug up again. But you asked for terms. Well, I'll be generous.

"You appreciate that I am strong enough to wipe you out with my next assault or, if that fails, the one after. But that doesn't really suit my purpose. Heroic last stands are something to avoid. They benefit the defeated, and make the victors look shabby. No, I don't want an heroic last stand. I want a humble surrender. Nothing big, mind you—just a gesture—and everybody's life will be spared."

"What gesture?" I asked.

Schwartz took a sip of his whisky before replying. "A small thing," he said. "I want Father Felix to take down that banner of his and hand it personally to me—barefoot. No. On his knees."

[139]

"On his knees?" I echoed. "Why on his knees?"

"That's what we're fighting about, my dear Weathers," said Schwartz. "Him and what he stands for. He has to surrender—humbly—"

"You can surely win on other terms," I countered.

"No," replied Schwartz. "On no other terms at all. I want the banner handed to me by the priest, barefoot, on his knees. I could hardly go back to my master without that. He will then be a prisoner. The rest, yourself included, may go free."

I made one last attempt. "There are a lot of your own men up there, heavily wounded, who will die if the fighting goes on," I said.

"It was I who let you save them," said Schwartz. "For a reason. They mean nothing to me. But there is nothing like the groans and cries of wounded men to demoralize a besieged garrison."

"That's diabolical," I said.

"Diabolical," he said with a smile. "You flatter me. No. It's not really diabolical. Just an old military wheeze— making your enemy defeat himself." He glanced at his wristwatch. "If the terms are accepted then the flag must be lowered. . . ." He hesitated and smiled at me. "There's really no hurry," he went on. "People should have plenty of time to consider such things. I will give you until tomorrow morning. No attack tonight. I know you will appreciate a good night's rest. But the flag must be lowered by sunrise; otherwise we attack again, and then there will be no terms at all. I will kill every man who falls into my hands. And I won't necessarily shoot him."

That was the message which I took back to the mission and relayed to Bomba and Father Felix.

"Schwartz cannot win," stated Father Felix unconcernedly. "If he destroys us, he loses. If he is driven back, he loses. His cause is doomed. There is no way he can secure victory." Not a word was said by either Father Felix or Bomba of surrender. The terms were rejected by silent assent as soon as they were heard.

I slept very well that night. It is indecision that disturbs our slumbers; uncertainty about what is going to happen. There was no uncertainty ahead now. We were all going to be killed, and that was quite a relief. The men manned the posts to the extent that they could, but I think many of them slept too. Before I turned in I saw Bomba go to the machine-gun nest atop the room and send down the crew and decided he was going to man the Vickers himself that night.

So I slept soundly and didn't awaken until a soldier shook me roughly at dawn shouting all the while, "They've gone. They've gone."

"Who's gone?" I asked. I thought for a jubilant moment that he was talking of Schwartz and his men.

"Father Felix and Bomba," he said. "They left during the night."

Chapter
Seventeen

THEY had gone indeed, incredible as the news seemed. One of the soldiers remembered seeing Bomba an hour or so before dawn—or rather passing a word with him in the dark. He had come down from the machine-gun post and said the gun was to be left unmanned. This struck the soldier as odd but it was not his business to protest.

We searched the mission thoroughly, calling for the two of them, but without success. And when my anger was white-hot against them for arrant treachery, I found, pinned to the wall of the priest's study, a note addressed to "Mr. Weathers." I opened it and read:

"Dear Mr. Weathers:

"I have done what I intended to do—given the world a chance to recover its conscience. A stand has been made, and a fine stand, upholding the dignity of man, the most beloved of God's creatures. You say the stand was used for propaganda purposes. But if this is so, then the fact that the stand had propaganda value shows that the cause of humanity still has some worth in the world and we have not yet lost our conscience and become another creature in human form. That is the great danger before us, the turning of Man into something inhuman.

"I have gone then to hand myself over to Schwartz, who may do with me what he will. I am an old man and a happy one who has properly used his mortal life. Bomba insists on accompanying me, though I would prefer that he remained. Please take down the banner yourself at dawn and burn it with honor as you would the flag of your own country—for it *is* the flag of your country though perhaps you do not recognize it as such at the present time. Tell the men what I have done and tell them that their names will be remembered in Heaven even if they are forgotten on earth. They are among the finest men Earth has seen and God will bless them.

Your Father in Christ
Felix Borowski."

Of the two of them, all that remained was the hen, searching anxiously around the compound for the comfort of Bomba's big feet. There was nothing to do but take down the flag and await the arrival of Schwartz. We burned the flag, as the priest asked, the men crowding around, some with blank faces and some with what might have been an expression of pain.

Schwartz took his time coming to us. It was midmorning before he and his men advanced toward the mission, and when he was within hailing distance the men were ordered over a loud-hailer to come out unarmed before the compound and stand there with their hands raised. Then Schwartz stupefied me by coming to the fore and shouting, "Where's the priest? Send him out barefoot with the flag."

"What the hell do you mean?" I asked. "He and Bomba surrendered to you hours ago."

"He did nothing of the sort," yelled Schwartz.

I gave him the priest's note and he read it through and then turned a smooth and knowing smile on me. "Well, well, well," he said. "What do you know? He ratted on you. After the agony in the garden, which you all shared, he did a bunk to avoid the crucifixion." He looked about at the surviving defenders of the mission and gave them the news in Swahili. They stared in disbelief at each other and then, terribly ashamed, they stared at the ground.

"What did you do with the banner?" demanded Schwartz.

"I burned it," I replied.

"A pity," said Schwartz. "I had intended making a shirt of it. Something to wear when I make a round of the bars. Like Prescott." He eyed the mission reflectively and his gaze rested for a moment on the Vickers with its sandbags on the roof. He gave an order to one of his officers and the handful of unarmed men who had surrendered were brought back inside the compound and left in a group. Schwartz mounted toward the machine gun, but it wasn't until he got to it and shouted for the captives to be huddled more closely together that I guessed what he was going to do.

"Don't!" I screamed. "It's murder!" But for answer Schwartz just turned his handsome face toward me, his fair hair glowing in the sunlight, and gave me a wave of his hand—a kind of "good-bye." The men looked about terrified, but found themselves hedged in by rifles. Schwartz disappeared into the machine-gun nest and I saw the snakelike barrel move just a fraction of an inch.

And then, with a tremendous explosion, the whole machine-gun nest blew up. Flames and smoke ripped out of the aperture and the whole thing disintegrated, fragments of wood and metal flinging down on us. Then the ammunition for the Vickers started exploding. I watched a whole belt of the stuff writhing all over the roof, bullets hailing about at random in every direction.

Everybody took cover. There was a lot of ammunition up there—.303 belt ammunition and grenades. The explosions, sometimes in chorus and sometimes solo, went on for several minutes.

Schwartz may have pretended not to know Bomba, but Bomba had known Schwartz. He had known him well enough to foresee that he would line up the men after they had surrendered and cut them down, unarmed, with the Vickers he hated. So he had booby-trapped the Vickers with a grenade, tying the firing pin to the barrel, so that as soon as it was moved, the grenade would explode. In the relative darkness of the gun nest Schwartz hadn't seen that it was booby-trapped. Schwartz had killed Prescott— Prescott's favorite weapon had killed Schwartz.

"An old military wheeze," Schwartz had said, "making the enemy defeat himself." Well, Bomba had known of it too.

By the time the explosions from the machine-gun nest were over, the remnant of Bomba's command had fled. They had used the confusion to scatter across the fields into the forest, into which the last two of them were disappearing when Schwartz's men got themselves together.

I alone had been fool enough to remain and I think I would have been killed but for the wounded. Some of them set up a terrible screaming and the soldiers burst into the makeshift hospital and found them there. They went fearfully around the beds, recognizing a comrade here and there. They said a word or two to those they recognized, but they held back from them, as if the bad luck they had met with might attach itself to them.

One of the wounded men pointed to me. I think he said I was the one who, with Father Felix, had brought him in. Or maybe he said that I had helped the priest take care of him. Anyway, after some more pointing in my direction, the soldiers went out, leaving me alone in the hospital. It seemed to me the wisest thing to stay there, and out of pure selfishness, rather than compassion for the men (in great fright, compassion is entirely out of the question), I got one man a drink of water and loosened a bandage on another. So I busied myself, hiding behind the injured, as it were, and when after a while no one else came, I looked out of the window.

They had gone.

They hadn't even stopped to loot the place. They hadn't formed any order of march or made a disciplined withdrawal. They had just gone, leaving me there in that ruined mission with a dozen men too heavily wounded to help themselves. So the whole aftermath of Father Felix's great stand was thrust upon my shoulders.

There was no question of my going off, first of all because I doubted I could survive in those wilds even if I was not killed by some trigger-happy soldier. Then, I couldn't leave the wounded. One of my Arab friends from those distant and long-forgotten dhows had told me that once, in a terrible tribal battle in the Atlas or some other mountains, when it had been necessary to leave some place in a hurry, they had cut the throats of all the wounded with a prayer to Allah. I had no belief in Allah and so I could not cut the throats of these men. Nor leave them. I was chained to them until somebody came to my relief.

For two days nobody came. Three more men died. I will skip the details of their burial beyond saying that I could not afford separate graves for them. I scooped out a hollow and shoveled some dirt over them, wondering how long the others would take.

The only other survivor was the hen. Two assaults on the mission, the mortar bombardments and the explosion of the machine-gun nest and ammunition had left the hen unscarred, its hennishness only slightly shaken. When I scooped out the grave for the dead men, the hen stood by, its head cocked to one side, hoping for worms.

But the hen saved me.

My temper, under strain, is always uncertain. At times I have magnificent control and at others I fly into a fury over the merest trifle. The hen supplied that trifle. It hopped up on top of the radiotelephone, which was so stupidly and stubbornly dead, and relieved itself into the works again. At this final display of animal contempt, I flung a tin mug out of which I had been drinking some muddy tea at it. The hen escaped with a tremendous cackling and fluttering and the mug hit the radiotelephone shrewdly. The hen darted out informing the world of my brutality, and when it had gone I heard from the radiotelephone a persistent hiss—like escaping steam.

It was working!

[*148*]

Having resisted the most careful ministrations of Prescott and of Bomba, its electricity, or its tubes, or its wiring, or whatever constituted its essence had been stirred into action by a good thump. That is often the case with electrical things.

I flew to it. It was definitely hissing. I knew enough to insert the jack for the earphones and look about for a button which said "Transmit." I found it and was shouting to be saved before I had even hooked in the microphone.

And then, restored to the world by the hen, I yelled a ridiculous appeal into the microphone. "Sacred Heart Mission. Sacred Heart Mission," I said. "For Christ's sake come and save me."

It was an old-fashioned set. You had to move a button to transmit and then move another switch to receive, carefully putting the transmit button to the "Off" position. But at last I mastered it and heard with incredible relief, "Sacred Heart Mission. Sacred Heart Mission. Maikap calling. We read you. Relief on its way. Repeat. Relief on its way."

I was so happy I didn't wait for any more. I just rushed out of the mission, with the earphones still on my head, cheering and shouting. I don't know what I said. I may have shouted "Hooray" or "Cockadoodledoo" or just yelled. But I recollected myself enough to rush into the hospital and shout to the men, "It's okay. We're all going to be saved. We're saved. We're saved."

They didn't understand the words, of course. But they heard me shouting and dancing around and saw the headphones still on my head so they knew that I had established contact. The man whose jaw had been shot away, and the side of whose head was now a glistening black balloon, raised his two fingers in the old Churchillian salute of victory.

I was so happy I even tried to make friends with the hen again. But the hen had had one keen, clear glimpse of the kind of creature I really am, and would have nothing more to do with me.

Chapter
Eighteen

COLONEL SELIM came for me the next day. In two hours'
flying time he had reached me from Maikap, flying not a
jet but a piston-engined plane. It was ridiculous. We had
been utterly and terribly isolated from all the world, and
then, there he was in his clean uniform, with the coffee
he carried in a Thermos still piping hot. He had flown a
piston plane because of its lower landing speed, which
permitted him to come down in the rough pasturage
around the mission. He circled the mission twice, debating
over the thornbushes and fences and hummocks of grass,
selected the best spot and down he came, steady and calm,
though with a series of heavy jolts to show how rough the
ground was.

He had brought a doctor and a nurse, medical supplies,
coffee, and for me two cans of cold American beer and a
pack of Camels.

"Where is Father Felix?" was one of his first questions, and when I told him that I didn't know, that Father Felix and Bomba had disappeared, he went immediately to the transmitter on the plane and relayed this news to Maikap —in fact to Utori. Then I was given the microphone, and I told Utori about the letter and the surrender and the utter disappearance of both Father Felix and Bomba.

"Schwartz was a long time coming to the mission after the flag was lowered?" he asked.

"Yes," I said. "Half the morning."

"Well then, he undoubtedly killed Bomba and Father Felix, and buried their bodies to make it look as though they had betrayed you. What do you think?"

"I just want to get out of here," I said. "This place is stinking with dead and wounded. It's the dirtiest, rottenest mess I've ever been in. I hope you got what you wanted out of it."

"Colonel Selim will fly you back immediately," he said. That was the end of our conversation.

We didn't leave immediately but awaited the arrival of a military helicopter bringing a small detachment of troops, though nobody really expected Schwartz's men to regroup and renew their attack on the mission. Colonel Selim also visited the hospital, examined the spot where the Vickers had stood, looked over the walls with their reinforcement of sandbags, shook his head over the ruin of the mission, visited the place where the dead had been buried and, coming to Prescott's grave, stood at the foot of it and gave a formal salute. I thought it only a military courtesy, but on leaving the grave he said, "Far, far better than Wigan." So he knew about that.

Before leaving he gave orders that the most thorough search was to be made for any trace of the bodies of Father

Felix and Bomba. Schwartz's camp was to be scoured, graves dug up and the forest around searched, for it was plainly important to prove that the two of them had been killed by Schwartz and had not deserted the rest of us.

It was late at night, then, when I reached Maikap and saw Utori. I saw him in a little reception room off his bedroom with but a curtain between the two. I think his wife was sleeping in the bedroom for I could hear deep breathing. Clad in light cotton pajamas and a dressing gown, he listened to my whole report. I can't pretend that it was a balanced report or that I had control of my emotions.

"I am aware," I said bitterly at the conclusion, "that we were all expendable from the start and just part of a propaganda piece aimed at getting support for your government. It's too bad that it has backfired, and that at the last heroic moment Father Felix disappeared."

"I won't deny the propaganda," said Utori. "The opportunity was there and I took advantage of it. That is why I am the head of a government. For the sake of my people I must use whatever weapons and tools are available. But I do not understand about Father Felix. He was not the man to run at the last moment. You have the note he wrote you?"

"No. It was blown up with Schwartz."

"That's bad," said Utori. "I think I know what happened. Schwartz was no fool. He wasn't going to supply the world with a martyr by publicly killing the priest or taking him captive.

"What he had to do was publicly shame him. Father Felix played into his hands there. You know honorable men are at a disadvantage when dealing with people like Schwartz. All Schwartz had to do was kill him and Bomba

[*153*]

and hide their bodies, and the world would suspect that at the last moment Father Felix had deserted his own cause and the very men who came to his defense. Not all the world, of course. But enough of the world to damage his reputation beyond recovery." He paused. I said nothing and in the silence listened to the chirping of the tree frogs and the sharp "pock" of a moth or a beetle colliding with the lights overhead.

"What do you think?" he asked eventually.

I was too tired to think. My mind was utterly weary of Father Felix, the mission, Blemi, Utori and the whole of Africa. "Right now I don't know what to think," I said. "I can only say that Father Felix said he was going to surrender to Schwartz and Schwartz said, in the presence of his own men, that he had never seen him."

"We'll find the bodies," said Utori. "We'll find the bodies if we have to dig up the whole of Blemi."

They never did find the bodies. They searched the forest and the clearing and they shot I don't know how many crocodiles in the river and opened up their stomachs, but they found nothing. The disappearance of the priest was a sensation for a few months, but then the world, having problems of its own, forgot about him. East Africa excepted.

I returned to Mombasa and for a while I didn't see anybody. Mrs. Blair kept people away from me and I spent most of my time down in the Arab *suk,* talking to the dhow pilots and captains who were utterly remote from the whole affair.

One day, however, Skinner turned up and was so insistent that I had to see him.

"They found him," he said. "Father Felix. Up in the

Cabo Hills. He's opened a new mission. I saw him myself. I could take you to him."

"No," I said. "You could not. And if Anano sent you, tell him this time it won't work."

"Anano," cried Skinner. "You don't think I have anything to do with him, do you? He's from Cyprus. He's not even an Englishman. His father ran a saddle shop." I didn't even offer Skinner the usual two days' hospitality. I just sent him on his way. Sure enough, though, a week later the whole of the East African village was buzzing with the report that Father Felix had returned and was running a mission in the Cabo Hills. Coulter on *The New York Times* even called me and asked whether I would check out the rumor and I told him I wouldn't.

"We never did get a satisfactory end to that story," he said. "It could be something as big as Stanley and Livingstone, you know."

"Well," I replied, "you find a reporter named Stanley and send him there. I'm staying here in Mombasa."

Other rumors followed. The next one came from Sister Elizabeth of the Cross, about whom I had almost forgotten. She called on me with her accompanying spirit and Mrs. Blair let them in without inquiry. Sister Elizabeth showed me a letter she had received from one of the helpers at the Sacred Heart Mission, whom Father Felix had ordered to leave the district in the face of the advance of Schwartz's men. She had shown it to Canon Kronk, who had suggested that she bring it to me. The letter said that Bomba's grave had been found and his remains identified, and that nearby there was another grave. It contained one of Father Felix's big Canadian hunting-type boots but no body.

"Sister," I said, "I am not about to buy a second resurrection story."

"Oh no," she cried. "I mean that the body must have been stolen."

"Look," I said, "it's possible Schwartz killed Father Felix and Bomba and buried their bodies to hide them. But if so, why would they come back and dig up Father Felix's body—carefully leaving behind one of his boots?"

"I don't know," she said, very upset. "I just thought I ought to show the letter to you. Canon Kronk thought you ought to see it."

So I saw Canon Kronk and asked him why he thought I ought to see the letter.

"Because you are responsible for all this rubbish in the first instance," he said with a snort. "Don't you think the Church has enough trouble on its hands without having to put down stories of mysterious priests wandering around in the African hills—ghost priests or zombies or some kind of mumbo jumbo. You know Schwartz killed Father Felix and you should have said so and made an end of the whole thing."

"I don't know that Schwartz killed Father Felix," I said. "Schwartz denied that he had ever seen him. There is no evidence to show what happened to him."

"Damnation," cried Canon Kronk. "What kind of a reporter are you, anyway? Do you mean to tell me you can't make up your mind between what Father Felix said and what Schwartz said? Let me tell you, my friend, the floor of hell is paved with the heads of people too fair-minded to choose between right and wrong."

It was then that the "empty grave" story started, and you will hear it still, I am sure, in some of those little hamlets scattered through the bush in those new African republics—the priest who rose from the dead to become East Africa's patron saint. Some of them even said he rose on the third day, which really made Canon Kronk wild.

To counterbalance the pious legends there were stories on the other side; stories to the effect that Father Felix had never been killed, but was living somewhere in Draki's territory, having, in return for his life, agreed to abandon Christianity and "go native." Stories that he had just deserted the men who had fought for him and disappeared to save his life. Quite a number of people believed these stories too. Once Robinson was thrown out of the Shamrock Club for flinging a glass of whisky in the face of a guest who said that Father Felix and Bomba had deserted in the end to save their own skins. Father Felix always had the most curious defenders.

I have put down the facts as I know them and, as you see, I write now merely of rumors and beliefs. I have no more facts, so you must make up your mind yourself about what happened to him.

There remains only a tremendous trifle more to add; something that for me completed the whole story.

A year or so later I went again to lunch with Grossheimer—the king salad, made of the heart of a palm tree (which kills the tree), was memorable. After lunch I had, of course, to view the latest additions to his beetle collection—two species which can eat through lead cable, and another which infects the bowels of children in India.

"That one there," said Grossheimer exultantly, "can emit a tiny jet of caustic gas when attacked—yes, they've invented gas warfare, just like us. And that's not a wasp. It's a beetle that looks like a wasp and gets into their nests to feed on their larvae."

I went away depressed and repelled as usual, and when

I was passing the Jesus fort, I met Mrs. Blair hurrying across the grass in the fading light.

"Oh, Mr. Weathers," she said. "I'm late. I hoped to get home before you."

"Where have you been?" I asked.

She hesitated. "The usual place, Mr. Weathers," she said. "This is Monday." And she hurried off.

It was a moment or two before I remembered the cemetery. For twenty years she had been going there every Monday, tending the grave of that drunken Scots engineer who had been her husband. She would be going there to the day she died.

Something thawed inside of me then, some terrible solid lump of cold that had formed during World War II and grown bigger with Korea and Vietnam and so many other things besides. Miraculously, it was gone. I think that for one moment I even had a glimpse of Father Felix—or was it Livingstone?—moving through the darting fireflies in the shadows under the trees, with that solar topee and that ridiculous Gladstone bag. But I knew enough not to shout out or follow. Instead, I went joyously to the Lusitania Club, where I bumped into Major Anano.

"You look happy," he said. "Good news?"

"I just realized he wasn't alone," I cried. "And he didn't lose. And it wasn't just propaganda for Utori. He can't lose. He's bound to win."

"Who?" demanded Anano.

"Father Felix, of course," I said. "And there weren't just two dozen blacks and Bomba with him. There were lots of people, everywhere. Always will be."

Anano considered me for a moment in his lardlike way while I looked about at the others in the bar, ready to embrace the whole club in my joy at being released from the ice. I recalled that at the bottom of Dante's hell it was all ice and the damned were buried up to their necks in it. I had been there myself for a long, long time.

"Who told you?" demanded Anano.

"Mrs. Blair," I replied. "Or maybe that drunken husband of hers, whose grave she is still tending. Or maybe Bomba and the hens. But Grossheimer is wrong. The insects are not going to win. We are going to win. Father Felix and Bomba and Mrs. Blair and Sister Elizabeth, and yes—Livingstone. All of us, the human beings." I was feeling a little light-headed and thought of the hens, for it was impossible to separate them from Bomba.

"Do you suppose there are Rhode Island Reds in heaven?" I asked.

"Haven't the foggiest," said Anano. He turned to the Parsee bartender and said solemnly, "Mr. Weathers could use a double."

I don't think he understood at all. On the other hand, he might have. You should never underestimate a British Political Officer.